BROTHER HARMONY
AND
SISTER CHAOS

BY STEPHEN GRESHAM

The blast of a shotgun woke him in the darkness just before dawn.

Bursting from the hovel, Easter ran with him deep into the boggy, piney woods until Harmony found what they were after. He tried to push Easter back, but she pried her way forward to where Orlin Ratcher lay, most of his head having been blown away. Methodically, Harmony went about wrapping the grotesque, shattered and bloodied head in strands of Spanish moss. Behind him, Easter chittered in the bird language she had used in conversing with her brother. When she had finished, Harmony slung the body over his shoulder, and they returned.

To a roaring mutation of his campfire.

And the sight of Micah cocooned within it, his eyes closed; he looked as if he were bracing against a strong wind. Easter screamed so intensely that Harmony's knees buckled.

He dropped the body of Orlin Ratcher on the ground and ran to the scene of self-immolation.

He had never seen anything like it.

Though he went about trying to crush out the flames, he knew it would do no good. Out of the corner of his eye he saw Easter dash into the hovel and return, holding something to her breasts. Then he backed away as she shrieked in agony and tossed the family Bible onto the fire, cursing.

But what precisely she cursed, Harmony did not know.

CONTENTS

BROTHER HARMONY
AND THE SHADOWS
THAT FALL ACROSS BEAUTY

Brother Harmony welcomed the color swatch of pink bog buttons and yellow star grass and the angel-winged whiteness of an egret in flight; he also smiled with satisfaction at the witchy cackle of two young gators bullying the duckweed surface of Wasp Heart Bayou for a spot of late morning sun. But he did not open to the coming of the women. For what *belonged* in Nahollo Swamp would not often arrive.

The east Alabama humidity was as thick as warm molasses. Blinking into that heavy air, Harmony thought of the somewhere bones of buried days. In his hours of the perpetually intransitive, he imagined—and believed he needed—nothing more. He composed sentences about himself in the third person, present tense: *he breathes, he dreams, he seeks, he longs. He no longer fears.*

And an afterthought: *he grieves.*

A giant, blue gum, black man he'd never seen before poled a johnboat steadily towards shore. Both women were dressed nicely as if going to or coming from church except this wasn't Sunday and the only holy sanctuary was the impenetrable cathedral of Nahollo Swamp.

A mother and daughter, he guessed, both dark-haired, thin and pale and lovely, the daughter just now leaving behind her teens. She carried a bantam chicken, red over black with a patina of gold on its neck. In one hand, the mother gripped wads of tissue that resembled gardenia blossoms; in the other she carried a grocery bag, cream-in-coffee colored, its contents unknown. When the black man nosed the boat in, he was told by the mother to wait. He seemed both sullen and filled with timidity.

Brother Harmony stepped from his long, low shack, and in a slow, weary voice said, "I don't do this no more." His head ached fiercely. He pointed vaguely to a sign near the door, plastic letters in black and white: *Spiritual Readings, Psychic Counseling, Spirit Connections, Past-Life Regressions, Future-Life Progressions.* Hanging from a hook just below that sign was another, this one addressed to additional services offered: *Clairvoyance, Psychometry, Palm Readings, Levitation, Automatic Writing, Etc.* Above the door, on a slab of gray-weathered cedar, a single sentence, all in caps, had been burned: *THERE IS NO DEATH.*

The woman trembled in response to Harmony's words.

"But I was told."

"No," said Harmony, "No more readings or counseling and such like. I'm gone from it."

The woman turned to stare at the daughter who was standing as still as a statue, her grip firm on the noiseless bantam.

"Sister Georgia Gresham sent us, sir."

Harmony's jaw clicked. He lowered his head and appeared to wince.

"Sister Georgia? That what you said?"

"Yes, sir. She spoke as you's the only one could help us. The only one."

Harmony muttered something his soul alone could hear. He removed his black, stovetop hat, much-worn, much-loved, and he wiped his brow with the sleeve of his long black cloak which hung from neck to heels like a priest's cassock. He brushed at the dust on the hat.

"How bad is it?"

Inside his abode, Harmony shooed Maybelline out of the way and ushered the two women into his inner sanctum through the entrance of multi-colored beads and behind a closed, surrounding curtain, black as soot. They approached a small, circular table. When Harmony lit a candle, the women found cypress chairs. On shelves to the far side of the area rested tarot decks, a crystal ball, a cooter shell, dice, and assorted other knickknacks of occult persuasion such as potions, goofer bags, fetishes, jujus, lucky-jacks, a skull, more beads and a mass of roots that seemed alive. Signs were posted here and there—one read *lux est umbra Die*, meaning "light is the shadow of God."

Opposite the women Harmony sat down in a cane-backed rocker he had fashioned himself. He noticed that the hands of both women possessed an exquisite loveliness, like ivory. But anger coiled in his stomach for inviting them in.

The mother, who chose not to introduce herself, cleared her throat.

"We're out of tryings," she said. "It's you our last chance."

"I'll say again, ma'am, that I'm gone now from all this. I'm sorry."

But then he saw it. That *something* in the woman's face reminding him that grief is an eyeless nightmare. That *something*. He saw that she was trying to expel a thing of anguish.

In the daughter's lap, the bantam rustled and gave forth a *puk* and a coo. The daughter grinned without joy.

"My name is 'Hally,'" she muttered.

Harmony nodded. The name reminded him of a bird and of a song. He glanced at the mother as if half alarmed. She released her grip on the paper bag and leaned forward.

"I must know how you see yourself as a man."

Her comment threw him off balance. He churned up a ball of saliva before he answered. Pain stabbed behind his right ear.

"*Isaiah* speaks of it."

"I must know, sir."

"In *Isaiah*, I read of myself—'And a man shall be as a hiding place from the wind ... and as the shadow of a great rock in a weary land.'"

"I am distant from the Bible, sir."

"No matter. That book never finds my deepest, oldest self. But I do, ma'am, see myself as secreting, at times, from all the elements, and I do assiduously avoid phantoms of energy indifferent to me."

She looked down and away and whispered, "I understand hiding."

Harmony studied her.

"Do you bring with you the needful task of healing violence?"

The mother, in a gesture of sorrow, placed one hand over her eyes.

Filling the sudden rise of silence, the daughter said, in a ghostly tone, "I have one, too." She lifted the bantam on to the top of her head, and as she did, the bird half squawked, ruffling its feathers in protest. A single feather brushed in gold spiraled to the floor.

Realizing her reference, Harmony removed his hat. He watched where the feather landed. He could feel the heat of the daughter's stare; her eyes raked over his shad-bellied waistcoat and his trousers strapped under his boots which were covered in the black, gleaming skin of a cottonmouth moccasin. With those eyes she stroked the beard connecting his chin to his sideburns; her examination felt the mustache-less upper lip and the remainder of his sad, wrinkled, furrowed face replete with a scattering of moles. Did she, as many others, see his resemblance to Abraham Lincoln? His tall, gaunt figure, large hands, his expression a most curious mix of grief, hope, despair and understanding?

Harmony forced himself to look again at the mother who met his eyes and found voice.

"Can you read her, sir? I have a lock of her hair?"

"No. No," he said. "I've stopped. My nerves have gone over."

But she continued.

"Is my daughter doomed by her beauty? That's what I've been told. Is my Hally to be cursed with disfiguring maladies?"

Hally, sweet Hally.

"Yes," he said. "I remember it now. The song about the mockingbird."

"Sir?"

Harmony turned to the daughter and smiled. She continued to hold the bantam on her head.

"The song," he said. "'Listen to the Mockingbird.'" He paused and looked just above the daughter. *"I'm dreaming now of Hally, sweet Hally, sweet Hally; ... And the mockingbird is singing where she lies."*

He stopped. Embarrassment rose in his throat. He reached down and retrieved the feather, rubbed it between his thumb and forefinger and closed his eyes as he experienced the caress of hope at the outset of an irresistible seduction. No need to brace himself for some vision of horror. He believed it was not to arrive.

The mother began to repeat herself.

"Last best chance."

She began to sob, and her tears smelled like rain.

"I don't see how I can help, ma'am. Beauty and deformities? Is there some kind of spell?"

He turned once again to the daughter whose breathing spoke to him. Without a word, she offered him the bantam. The settled *puk puk* of it caused him to chuckle. He started to reach out for it, but his hands felt as heavy as steel. He hesitated.

"You wish me to take it?"

The daughter's eyes suddenly matched the color of her pale skin.

"Can you see what we mean?" she said.

Harmony raised the feather.

"I see only the wonder of this. The beauty of it." He began again to rub the feather; he looked from daughter to mother and back again. "You are troubled and have brought your suffering. If you stay, expect the truth."

"My name is 'Hally,'" she said.

"Yes, I know."

The mother stopped crying, yet whimpered like some animal in deep distress.

The daughter pushed the bantam towards Harmony.

"It's here," she said.

The flesh of her fingers blackened and instantly enlarged like the blossoming of a dark flower; the shape of them acquired the angle of lobster claws with a force becoming its own mystery. Then, razor-sharp, they closed upon the bantam and ripped and tore, sending eerie screams rather than squawks out beyond the shack into the bayou. Wings flapped, beating helplessly. Blood sprayed. It speckled the daughter's chin and moistened the corners of her mouth. She licked at it as if it were a treat. Some of the blood drizzled upon Harmony's trousers and his boots, and as he stared at the unfolding horror he looked like a man who was a long ways from understanding. His hands drew up like dying spiders. He lifted them to his side as if weighing emptiness.

As the blood spread and created rivulets and pools, the daughter seemed, strangely, to have risen from the glimmering fluid. The brutality of the scene descended upon Harmony, then roiled up in him like vomit. When the violent actions ceased, when the bantam had been clawed into a dozen or more gobs of flesh and feathers and entrails and bones, the daughter began to hum to herself some child's song from an old dead time. Her fingers of knife-point, dark stone clicked together like castanets. She rocked back and forth as she hummed; her blood-ringed mouth floated as if detached, seeming to Harmony to hover just above the candle flame.

Whispering a litany of apologies, the mother calmly went about cleaning up the carnage, gently placing remnants of the bantam into the grocery bag as if she were selecting fruit, and, with what appeared to be a towel, she mopped at the patches of blood, and when she finished she rose and led her daughter away.

Shaken to his core, Harmony followed them. In his softest voice, he asked the woman if she would return tomorrow. He could think of nothing more to offer. He sensed that his legs were about to fail him.

"Yes," she said.

At the end of the day Harmony sat on his front step watching a sunset the color of a ripe peach. Maybelline, an orphaned raccoon, pregnant and needy, sat in his lap and sought, with paws and tongue, for the bottle of strong homebrew Harmony was guzzling. The liquor was the proud creation of Merlin and Mance Gresham, the most skilled moonshiners in the whole of Nahollo Swamp. They named each of their batches—this one dubbed "Mule Piss," not entirely as sardonically as one might think.

The insects of twilight chorused.

Harmony thought of the nearly comatose Sister Georgia who had, years ago, trained him to be a medium, she being the most masterful at the practice he had ever known. Was she trying in her inimical way to entice him back to his calling? He vowed to resist. He swigged from the bottle. Maybelline chittered until he allowed her to lick the rim.

"You want all your damn little coonies to be drunks? What the hell kind of mama-to-be are you?"

Maybelline's tongue worked with both impunity and indifference.

Harmony realized that in his other hand he still had the single feather from the bantam.

"Shit," he muttered.

Passing directly in front of his shack was a johnboat poled by a young, black creature named *Sway de Rille*. He never escaped being stirred by the sight of her, the wildness of her, the bronzed shapeliness of her body, the coiling fall of her long, black hair like singed wisteria vines. Riding with her was her protector— her familiar?—a rare, Florida panther she called "Lilith," the eyes of the cat bluer than ever Paul Newman's were. He waved at the fascinating woman, and when he did, the feather spun away.

She slowed her boat.

"I know your secret, Brother Harmonica! Do you know mine? Brother Harmonica, have you learned that poisons grow in the dark?"

Her smile sprang from madness, her laughter originated in a depraved heart.

"Sway of my desire," he returned. "I've found that what is done for love always takes place beyond good and evil."

She moaned loudly.

"Stop reading so many books or the organ of your manhood will shrink into a slug or a minnow. Do you hear me, Brother Harmonica?"

"Yes, but I don't heed you, for you're only an illusion, a figment of Nahollo."

Her laughter trailed her into the gloaming before rising into the first stars. The big cat snarled, then screamed like a woman giving birth to some hideous monster of the approaching night.

Harmony went inside to listen to music and drink some more so that he could forget about his morning visitors. He knew that he should eat something, but he wasn't hungry. He set out a pan of milk for Maybelline. With another bottle of the Greshams' best, he spread out his CDs of blues and old rock & roll, a collection of vintage stuff: Magic Slim, Rufus Thomas, Howlin' Wolf, Johnny "Guitar" Watson, Etta James and, two of his special favorites, Bo Diddley and Chuck Berry. As the only white boy years and years ago to frequent *Took's*, a juke joint operated by one of his surrogate fathers, Joe Eddie "Talkin' Man" Took, he had received the elegant dogma of the blues, then progressed to rock & roll.

Sitting akimbo on the floor, a lantern for light, he fed his CD player and listened to Chuck Berry duck walk his way through a jungle of steaming lyrics. But his thoughts wandered—to the mind-numbing execution of the bantam, to the horrifying morphing of Hally's lovely hands.

Oh, God.

And the suffering mother? How to help her?

Only one way.

His head throbbed.

Lantern in hand, he crossed the dog trot to the room occupied by Sister Chaos who lived with him rent-free, no exchange of fringe benefits of the usual kind except that, in the days of his practice as a spiritual medium, he would often ask her for advice when a patron presented him with a hard mystery. A sign on her door, one she had stolen somewhere, spelled out *Dead End* in black letters against an orange background. Harmony smiled shyly at the shadowy woman's sense of humor.

Would she be gone?

He put his ear to the door. All that he truly knew of her was that she slept during the day, roamed all night, read trashy, true-crime books and magazines and listened to jazz recordings. He cleared his throat, leaned down and put his lips to the keyhole.

"I need your assistance."

When he satisfied himself that she might be listening, he told her everything. Every detail of moment-to-moment futurity regarding the mother and daughter and the bloody scene he had witnessed. He concluded with a harsh whisper: "What can I tell the mother to do? Is there a way to help her?"

He waited.

Gradually a weird ventriloquy of sounds swirled around him before the voice of Chaos seemed to emerge from his chest. He listened carefully. Drank in the words. Thanked her. Cautioned her to be careful on her nightly trek.

Knew that she wouldn't.

He tried to sleep.

His headache worsened.

Before, at last, some imagined, ancient run of blues from an out of tune piano carried him from his sleeplessness into oblivion.

A gash of daybreak.

He brewed a pot of strong coffee and sopped a cathead biscuit in a saucer of milk with Maybelline begging for her share at his pant's leg. He heard the golden scream of an unknown bird and the whisper of Spanish moss, and he could smell the smoke of genuine suffering.

It was on its way.

"Well, God damn," he said to himself.

Maybelline stole out of sight with his second biscuit.

More than an hour passed before the woman returned with her daughter bound to the bottom of the johnboat in heavy chains draped around her neck and shackling her hands and bare feet. The giant black man, his forearms bleeding as if they'd been scratched or clawed, poled in a feckless daze.

"Will you lose her?" said Harmony as he helped to secure the boat.

"No," said the mother. "She's lost until she's found."

"I know how that is, ma'am."

"What do you have experience of in that?" she said, sounding doubtful.

Harmony, taking her arm and ushering her up to his shack, murmured, "I lost a boy. A son. Or maybe he's hidden. Maybe he, too, will be found."

"Can you help a godforsaken woman, sir?"

His headache raged and bit at his brain.

"I must," he replied. "It's all comin' back."

Behind the curtain, a new candle flickering, Harmony passed along the enigmatic solution Sister Chaos had implanted. He spoke in a gentle, hypnotic voice. He watched for the woman's reaction.

"That how it has to be?" she said, new wrinkles crow footing out from the corners of her mouth. She blinked as if imagining what could not possibly be imagined.

"In these matters, ma'am, it rings like a truth. But it is a desperate one. These awful maladies demand a high price. Think on it. Come back at sundown. Make sure you bring your daughter."

She nodded. Got up to leave. Hesitated.

"Has to be ... *that* way?"

"Think on it, ma'am. Pray. Or what have you. Whatever gets a body through."

He watched mother, daughter and black man pole away as the morning sun bore down, and he wondered what the dark enchantments of womanhood would bring to bear.

In his rocking chair, Harmony dozed.

Mid-afternoon, a thunderstorm swept through as was common in Nahollo. It woke him. He stood at his door and watched the fury of it; he breathed in the cooler air and sighed with the slight relenting of his migraine. Words tossed about in the part of his brain that juggled: words such as *ebbed, bloomed, rocking, weeping*. Why those particular words he couldn't have said.

When the storm had lifted, he spoke to the departing thunder: "I hope they do not return," referring, of course, to the women. He did not want to see what would have to be seen.

But in the heart of the stillness of the waning afternoon, they found their way. It seemed to Harmony that the black man had shrunk, though he knew it must be a trick of the light. The face of the mother, stony and expressionless, could be read only as the end product of resignation—the sight of it made Harmony's stomach judder. The daughter sat, sans chains, her hands hidden in her armpits. As Harmony gazed upon her, a shadow from nowhere fell across her eyes, darkening an evident hopefulness there.

Ever so softly he whispered the word, "Welcome," to them.

Behind the curtain once again, the threesome sat like broken spokes in the wheel of the candlelight. Restless, obviously eager for what wanted to come, the mother straightened herself and said, "Well, tell us the final thing, and we'll get this over with, sir."

He nodded soberly.

The beauty of the daughter's face, hidden or buried beneath the violence in her blood, arose tentatively, then, as if reaching some predetermined limit, ceased. Disappointed, Harmony closed his eyes. The pain in his head bugled suddenly, causing him to gasp.

"Sir?"

When the mother, concerned, reached for him, he opened his eyes and, seeing her lovely fingers, took them and guided them to her daughter's wrist.

"Here," he said. "Here. Hold on tightly and breathe in, open yourself, open yourself."

And she did.

The malformations closed over the woman's flesh with barely a second's hesitation—like a blue-black armor of claws and horns. The woman shrieked; the daughter quietly wailed, a keening of both sadness and relief.

The essence of the mother oozed out of her, sans will, sans life, like toothpaste worming out of its tube. The new surface of hard, clattery material pulled her within it. Her bones cracked and popped, and the sound of the crushing was horrific. It continued almost in slow motion until the woman's dark shelled remains were no larger than a basketball.

The daughter, more capaciously beautiful with each passing moment, grew profoundly still as her realization of her mother's sacrifice took hold. Harmony could hear her breathing. Saw tears. Saw something that must have been love. He felt himself shuddering, and from an unknown place inside him, a flame of new understanding ignited.

Refusing his help, the daughter lifted the remnants of her mother, thanked him and left the area. Harmony blew out of the candle, knowing that the old belonging had fully returned. He would no longer be able to resist those who suffered and would come petitioning for his help.

He watched as the astonishingly beautiful daughter carried her burden down to the johnboat where the large black man helped her aboard. They were losing light. Amber dots from the distant eyes of trolling gators drew closer as the man pushed the boat away from the shore.

Harmony saw more shadows gather at the outline of the daughter.

But then he turned away and did not watch his visitors depart.

BROTHER HARMONY
AND THE VOICES OF DAWN

"You got no choice. It be in your blood, son. Get down and suffer with it to glory. That's what *I'm* sayin'."

Brother Harmony felt the uncomfortable wisdom of those words. His old friend, Took, spoke from a heart as ancient and unchallengeable as the wind.

"You want me to destroy myself?"

Took threw his liver-spotted, bald head back and laughed. He puffed on his cigar and rapped his cane upon the concrete that had once been a dance floor in the intimate fierceness of his juke joint. His huge stomach stretched suspenders to the breaking point; his ninety-four-year-old body was as creaky as his rocker. But his mind burned with lyrical strangeness.

"Son, when you lost your wife, when you lost your boy, you gone on then and ended all you ever was. Seems you got nothin' left to lose. Ain't I right?"

"I don't want this."

"You've done been called back. That's the whole thing."

A light rain fell beyond the dirty, smeary front glass of Took's. Harmony had come to Carinthia, a dead town on the edge of the swamp, to visit Sister Georgia, but had found her floating motionlessly in a deep coma. Her attendant, Jamesia, a midnight woman, believed that Sister Georgia was nearing her transition from this life into the *Summerland* of the beyond. Harmony refused to believe it. Before he left the dear, old woman's bedside, he leaned down and whispered into the leathery deformity that was her ear, "Please send your spirit to guide me. I'm all the way shaken. I'm fallin' away."

Disappointed, he sought out Took and told him of the mother and her daughter. He wanted answers; Took simply reminded him that the dark corners of existence were filled with mysterious shadows—just accept it.

"I don't think I can."

"This here ain't about choice."

And that's when Took mentioned a situation he felt Harmony should consider responding to. Took's grandson, DayQuan—nicknamed "Toe Jam"—had experienced a decisive encounter near Hog's Eye Run, a creeklet bleeding into a swirling, backwater pool of Lake Nahollo.

It was not a safe place.

There, DayQuan, a veteran of the fighting in the Middle East who roamed Nahollo in camouflage, carrying an assault rifle, had heard strange voices yesterday at dawn. A family of swampers claimed to him that they were victims of a vampiric Spanish moss and that while there was no hope for them, they wanted to try to save their small boy from their same fate. They had hidden him in the Cat Bells cave system.

Even though the family had refused to let DayQuan see them, he had gotten a fleeting glimpse of the face of the father, a sight too hideous for him to put into words.

"All that's bullshit," Harmony had exclaimed. "For years there've been stories of vampiric moss in Nahollo—stories, nothing more."

Took had paused to puff thoughtfully on his cigar.

"My grandson's crazy, but he ain't a liar." His voice thickened as he reached for the most vulnerable part of Harmony's emotions. "Somebody needs to be that little boy's savior."

Shaking his head vigorously, Harmony felt anger claw up in his throat.

"I just went through this, Took. God damn it, I won't do it again."

Took nodded.

"I see. I see. So, you're sayin' you jus' plain don't give a shit?"

"What am I supposed to do? Should I pack 'em up a bunch

of garlic and wolf's bane and a Mason jar of holy water? Could be this is just one big joke."

"Am I laughin'?"

"Look, if the situation has some truth to it, you know that nonsense from vampire books wouldn't help none. I don't have the kind of real and honest protective powers it would take."

"Use roots. You got 'em. Ghost weave 'em. Call on your Chaos woman for her darkness."

"They'll have to be some damn, fuckin' strong roots. You know that, don't you?"

Took smiled victoriously. Blew a trail of blue smoke.

"I do, sir. I do," he said, rocking back into the music of his long-suffering moments, the arthritis in his joints and the ugly spots on his lungs.

Harmony hugged the old man and planted a wet kiss on his misshapen skull.

"I hate you for this," he murmured.

It could have been a figment of his imagination, the angel perched high in a moss-draped, tall cypress, the knees of which were polished to a spit shine, enchanted, silent, timeless.

Against his better judgment, Harmony had ventured miles away from Wasp Heart Bayou into the bitter waters of Lake Nahollo, pressing up, pre-dawn, to the mouth of Hog's Eye run. For company, he had a high beam flashlight and Maybelline who sniffed at the air, at the warm, dark cave essence of sleep while the distant stars of summer prepared to retreat.

Harmony steadied the boat.

I have forgotten all my days of not being terrified.

The untraceable origins of anxiety spawned doubts, fears.

The angel morphed into a massive, great horned owl and turned its eyes away from his approach.

Spittle of mist touched Harmony's face like something unseen, like something not physical but rather a projection from the ageless practice of trying, via wild talents, to help those who could not help themselves. At least to attempt to give them hope.

And what is hope?

No, not a thing with feathers, he reasoned. It was a pearl in a shell of doubt waiting for a diver to bring it up into the world of those who must keep trying. Yes, that sounded trite. But so be it. Some things were simply difficult to imagine—try, for example, fixing thoughts of Jesus as an old man.

At the far end of the run, haunted voices, in a seemingly helpless gesture, were being tossed out into the ever-thickening mist. Harmony switched on his beam. Maybelline chattered, cowering at his ankles.

"Who's there?"

A single voice, muffled, not quite human, responded. It appeared to be coming from under water.

"Put out your light, please."

So he did.

He edged his boat into the run and, once again, steadied it.

"I'm told you need help. What's going on?"

The pause was alarmingly long.

"Something is … *feeding* upon us. The moss, we believe."

Harmony could feel long strands of it above him like flags limp on a windless day, and yet the plants seemed to be guarding the narrow path of water.

"I want to help. If I can, I want to help."

"Dear God. No one can … except. We've hidden a boy. Our son."

"I believe I might be able to get him away from here. Away from … the *moss*. But I want to see you."

"No! No, no, you must not! Dear God, no!"

"Can you tell me about it—about what's happened?"

Another excruciatingly long pause.

"You see, … it's in our blood now." Then the voice dissolved briefly as if being strangled. When it regained a steady flow, it issued these words: "Do you have a way? A plan?"

Harmony felt his knees trembling as he stood and leaned heavily upon his stob pole.

"I'll prepare roots. Protective roots."

Though he was unsure, he told the family that he would hang a wreath of roots on a cypress branch tomorrow night. They were to retrieve it and to place it around the neck of the boy. At that point, they could load him into a boat—he must be alone—and let it drift to the mouth of the run.

"He's a fine boy," said another voice, this one possibly female.

Harmony hesitated a few moments.

"Boys are. Yes, I'm sure he is."

And then the voices evaporated as if he had only dreamed them.

The vandal root was foul smelling, an odorous mixture of decaying vegetation and road kill. Next were strands of masterwort and bat weed, the latter a strong substance for cleansing and uncrossing. Woven together, they would forge a powerful protectant, or so Harmony believed.

Then, with a long rope of bridal briar he ghost-weaved the concoction until it shaped itself into a wreath. In his hands, it felt almost alive, serpentine and as magical as he could make it.

Except for one thing more.

At the door to the private quarters of Sister Chaos, he explained the situation he had given himself to. He placed the wreath of roots on the doorknob. He asked for her to empower it. He reminded her how much he believed in her wild talents. Then he returned to his part of the shack and listened to Bo Diddley and drank "Mule Piss" until his head buzzed and his throat flamed. Over and over he listened to Diddley's "Ride on Josephine":

Ride on Josephine, ride on
Ride on Josephine, ride on
Ride on Josephine, you got a runnin' machine
A-baby, baby, ride on Josephine, baby ride on

Two hours later he stood and stared at the wreath hanging where he had placed it on the doorknob. He could tell that it had been moved. That realization made him shiver with a secret gladness. The wreath was oddly moist and gave off an odor with which he was unfamiliar. Into the keyhole he murmured, "Thank you."

Then the night called him to his task.

The water lilies of Lake Nahollo whispered against the side of his boat, the sound louder in the blackness than he thought might be possible. He had left Maybelline at the shack. His stob pole seemed to weigh a ton. His high beam rested where the light could skim over the surface of the water and the vegetation.

Living things watched.

A monkey-faced owl cooed in deep, eerie gutturals. Pairs of eyes, curious, fierce fires glowing, floated near, and of those gators, a young, large bull issued a drawn-out hiss, ominous and chilling. He heard the *burrumf* of frogs and the distant scream of a predatory cat—could it have been Lilith?

It was hard not to be fascinated by the dangers and unspeakable terrors of Nahollo Swamp, and yet he went about his business quickly, looping the wreath over a cypress branch even as he noticed the thick mass of moss overhead. He poled away, docking at one of several islands in the lake, one known as Cooter Island, and there he found himself waiting once again.

It was not a time for paralyzing fear.

But sounds were amplified: bird calls, insect hummings and the dry rustle of deer nibbling at berry bushes. To distract himself, he drummed up a snatch of an old swamp song, one his family of spiritualists would call *purely pretty*:

> *He turned his face upon the wall*
> *And death was in him dwellin',*

No, *not* pretty—purely *bleak*. Not what he needed.

The long hair beneath his top hat was sweating. The wild majesty of Nahollo Swamp at night clutched invisible hands at his throat. Time passed, how much he did not know. He poled to Hog's Eye run where jungle sidings of vegetation as tall as the screen of the nearly-gone-forever drive-in movies loomed. Along side the edges of the lake were vast boglands of petrifying logs and cyclical swamp-burned stumps and deep pools of stagnant water where moccasins liked to hook up in grotesque mating balls.

He speared his light.

He could see that the wreath was gone.

The boy must be on his way.

And Harmony felt the great *missingness* of his wife and son. His son, "Aidan." They called him "The Kid."

His wife, "Marlena." Harmony carried the scent of both of them. When, he wondered, would those scents dissipate?

He waited.

Flags of Spanish moss unfurled above the run. But he had confidence in the roots.

When he saw the small boy floating towards him in a boat, he was stunned by the innocence and beauty of the face and the dark, curly hair, the child shirtless, the wreath hanging heavily around his neck.

The boy was no more than thirty yards from freedom.

Harmony kept the beam above his head so that he would not be blinded.

"Be brave. Be brave," he suddenly, impulsively called out to him.

The wreath appeared to be uncomfortable.

"What is your name, son?"

His voice like a frayed ribbon fluttering weakly, the boy said, "Jolus."

Harmony nodded. His heart beat wildly.

"I'm a friend, Jolus. You'll be safe. I'm a friend."

The night ticked down.

Until an instant of membranous meaning. Harmony saw it begin with a glow coming from deep within the eyes of the boy like candlelight in a Halloween pumpkin.

"You'll be safe."

But Jolus knew.

He looked up.

Screamed.

And tore the wreath from around his neck.

The tangle of vining moss threaded down and, with a macabre precision, began to wound under the boy's chin and to encircle his throat.

Harmony cried out until his lungs burned.

He saw the boy's hands reach for the vines of moss. Heard gurgling and a panic of gasps. Watched the body lift free of the boat. Watched it jerk. And dance. Then judder. Then juke. Then rise into the upper reaches of the cypress.

Harmony poled madly to the sight of the lynching, but even the feet of the boy rose well beyond his grasp.

"Jolus!" he shouted again and again.

Then, seeing a fresh snaking of moss, he turned and poled away to save himself.

Later, as he returned to his shack, Harmony saw no meaning in another sunrise, and he never again heard the distraught family and their voices of dawn.

The end of all things.

All things ended there.

BROTHER HARMONY
AND THE HOUSE OF THE RISING DEAD

She was a light that made his world believable.

"Can you stay till morning?" she said, and the taste of hopefulness in her voice quietly thrilled him, bringing him, momentarily, back to life, back from a dark cell of horror to which he had been sentenced. Or had sentenced himself.

"If you'll have me do so."

"Alan Wayne Trapman, you know I will."

Her name was "Chosen," and she ran a place known as "Chosen's Community House," in a run-down, gray=weathered, two-storied hulk of a building where she welcomed those fallen on hard times, those in need of necessities, mostly women and the gypsy-like children who accompanied them. The establishment was something of a combination of Goodwill, Salvation Army, safe house, and out-in-the-sticks doc-in-a-box. If any woman within twenty miles of Nahollo Swamp longed for the practical commiseration of another woman, she would likely end up at Chosen's door. And, most definitely, not be turned away.

Alan Wayne Trapman.

Brother Harmony smiled at hearing someone call him by his real name, though that man, in so many ways, had ceased to exist.

"Could we maybe go somewhere and talk?" he said.

Chosen, who was sorting through Hefty bags of donated clothing, glanced around. While she had a couple of younger women and one older, retarded woman as helpers, she rarely left her post. "I'm the Ole Miss and then some," she often said. But before she could respond, Harmony was attacked by her two daughters, Violet and Viola.

"Uncle Alan, are you here?" they exclaimed in unison.

Twenty fingers used his face as a keyboard. Two bodies as one hugged at his waist.

"I think maybe I am. How you rascals been?"

"Fine," they said, again in unison.

They took turns trying to put on his top hat.

"You bein' good 'n fine help to your Mama?"

"Yes, sir. Yes, sir," they chanted through a swirl of giggles.

He was not their uncle, but he adored them. He would have felt sorry for them, but Chosen would not, even for a moment, allow such a thing. They were conjoined twins—fastened at the temple, and they were quite pretty in matching green print dresses and a Medusa-sprouting of green ribbons in their long-ish, red hair—Chosen's hair. They were thirteen.

Prying her daughters from Harmony's fatherly presence, Chosen said,

"You girls go on back and watch the little bitty ones so they don't wander off to the swamp and get gobbled up for lunch by the gators."

"Oh, Mama!" they chorused, somewhat alarmed or repulsed, then danced away.

Chosen reached for his hand.

"I'm on borrowed time," she said, "but you're lookin' like you could use a friend."

They followed a pine straw path to a slough fifty yards behind her building, and there they sat on cypress stumps, and the still backwaters created a mirror world where a young snowy egret and its reflection fed in shadow-strewn light. Spanish moss tumbled down on either side of the bird.

It was a lovely *temenos* of a spot.

Though Harmony stared at the moss with eyes of disdain.

"Can I speak at you about what's been going on?" he said.

She smiled, her pale, freckled face betraying the fact that she had recently turned forty. Beauty held there, and yet had faded some, and she was thinner than the last time he'd seen her, almost a wisp of a woman except for largish breasts and a nice, rounded ass.

"Isn't that why we're here? 'Course, if you'd rather toss me down on the pine straw and take advantages, I won't put up a fight."

He pulled her close and tugged playfully at her cascade of red hair tied in a ponytail.

"I'd damn sight rather do that than wallow in my confession."

She removed his top hat and kissed him almost full on his lips, and he groaned as if he'd just been given a transfusion of sexual energy. She looked too far into his eyes and said, "Word has it you're back with the spirits—back bein' a medium, where you belong."

"I know," he said, "you've always believed that about me."

He unloaded every moment of his experiences with the mother-daughter and with the boy, Jolus, and he fought tears that embarrassed him, and when he finished, he lost his grasp on words and just shook his head.

She caught his face in her hands and said,

"You helped save the daughter, and you tried to save the boy. Main thing is, you're living again on the side of those suffering. *Your* terms. Using *your* gift." She studied his face as if prelude to a diagnosis. "You still gettin' those headaches?"

He nodded.

"It's like there's a fuckin' little nest of razor blades behind this right ear."

She rubbed at the area and for a moment the pain completely relented.

They loved each other. But too much probably to ever marry.

"Maybe you're dippin' your bill in that Gresham hooch more 'n you should," she said, teasingly.

He smiled.

"Could be. Or could be that having grown up in Nahollo generates some God damn nightmares."

She shook her head in mock exasperation.

"Trapman, you know it's not where you were born that matters—it's where you were *reborn,* and I don't mean in the 'I've found Jesus' way, but more the location of your real change."

"Initiation into an authentic self, you mean?"

"I do."

"At Wasp Heart Bayou," he murmured. "It's like being in the heart of stillness. It happened there."

He didn't have to say anything about place. She knew. She had been raised in the swamp in a primitively religious family, a cult of Bible-breathing, wild, rough folks who handled snakes and believed they could raise the dead. At fifteen, Chosen had been forced to marry "Harlan," a distant Haggardy cousin; his rotten seed led her to two miscarriages and then the birth of Violet and Viola. A spell later, during a "holiness with signs following" service he was bitten on the cheek by a large, eastern diamondback he had taken up. In less than an hour that side of his face swelled to twice the size of the other—he lived six days and on the seventh he rested permanently, having suffered more than anyone had ever witnessed. God didn't bother to save him.

His two brothers, harsh, mean, cruel devils, continued to run the church and began to abuse the women and children of the congregation. The church itself was known as *The House of the Rising Dead* because "Henry" Haggardy believed God had given him the power to restore life to the dead, and he exercised his miraculous talent in the dark, opprobrious basement area called "The Lazarus Room." Though he could point to no case of his restoration powers having been successful, he never lost faith, and, eventually, was arrested for digging up bodies from cemeteries in the area. "Haggar" Haggardy also succumbed to an obsession of sorts when, as a result of a decisive encounter with what he called a "lizard man" deep in the swamp, he abandoned both the church and his senses to spend the remainder of his days seeking out the fantastic creature, apparently dying before ever proving its existence.

As the years passed, The House of the Rising Dead, its spiritual mission having been aborted, fell into disrepair. Chosen claimed the building, restored it somewhat and reached out to help others without the aid of serpents, cryptoids or the Bible.

"You'll get through this," she said.

And in that moment he found in her the sympathy he

had needed. His affection for her almost overwhelmed him. They talked on, companionably, in a symbiosis of words, and Harmony suspected that was the only way a man and a woman should ever converse.

That night they made love.

At first light, with her warm, naked and deliciously desirable body pressed against his, Harmony heard the blues shuffle quietly out of his soul; he knew, of course, that they would return, but he was never sorry to see them leave.

Chosen stirred and pushed up to where her full, firm breasts rested against his hairy chest.

"That Chaos woman still hangin' 'round your place?"

"She is. You jealous?"

"Should I be?"

"Don't see why." He hesitated. "At times lately she's been helpful."

"Okay, if you believe it."

"I don't beg her to stay, if that's what you mean."

She fell silent. He listened to her breathing and to the sleepy pulse of blood in her temples.

"Any of all this about 'Aidan'?" she said.

He sighed deeply.

"It's *always* somewhere along the way about Aidan. About loss and failure."

"Failure how?"

He spoke into her hair.

"I mean, don't you see? I mean, if I really, truly have extra powers—including psychometry—why the hell's it not possible for me to lo-cate him? At least his ... well, his body? Something of him to let us know what...."

His tongue refused to issue more.

They held each other a few minutes longer, wrapped in flesh and silence and stolen satisfaction and a grudging acceptance of so many things that could not be changed.

"How 'bout I fix you a decent breakfast?" she said.

"I won't oppose you there, ma'am," he responded.

After breakfast, he listened to Violet and Viola chatter on

about their ambition to become country western singers, claiming they could sing as well as Taylor Swift any time of the day. Harmony had never heard of any singer named Swift, but he loved seeing a sparkle in the eyes of Chosen's girls.

In the early hours of the day, he stayed out of the moment-to-moment futurity of the operation; he couldn't help noticing, however, that Chosen, quiet and distracted, had something on her mind. He had taken up hammer and nails to piece together new book shelving for a batch of donated paperbacks when she approached him with a cup of coffee.

"Sweetheart, I've got a big ole favor to ask."

He grinned. Then sipped at the hot liquid to burn at the cold serpent of anxiety beginning to coil in his stomach.

"What's her name?"

She smiled and punched at him gently.

"'Mandolin'—we call her 'Mandy.'"

He paused to look into the bottomless pools of hope in Chosen's eyes.

"How bad is it?" he said.

Her jaw flinched. She glanced away and blinked rapidly.

"Seems it's a *birth turning*. It's far gone down the road a desperate thing."

"Is she here? This moment, is she here?"

She nodded.

"Down in 'The Lazarus Room.'"

"She believes I can help?"

"I convinced her you could."

"A *birth turning* is a hard mystery."

Again she nodded.

"Mainly, she just has to know what she's carrying?"

"Christ, has she even seen a doctor?"

"You know she hasn't."

The scene declared a single, naked bulb situated over two white, plastic chairs from Wal-Mart. Though the young woman was twenty, she looked all of fifty and drained of vitality. When she shifted in her chair, she began to shiver like a wet dog. Harmony smiled and whispered something inaudible. Timidly she raised her face, and he sketched, for the sake of memory, how empty and fragile it was, wispy, utterly feeble. Her hair was straight and black, and there were bags under her eyes that appeared to have been smudged with lampblack; her eyebrows were like skid marks; they seemed to have been drawn on with a black crayon by some school child. She was likely six or seven months pregnant.

"Chosen says you'd like my help."

Her eyes said yes, and then, in a voice scarcely a whisper, she said, "Do there be spirits, sir?"

"Yes, ma'am. I learned of them in *I Samuel* where it reads, 'And the Spirit of the Lord will come upon thee, and thou shalt prophecy with them, and shalt be turned into another man.'"

"Have you been?"

"Ma'am?"

"Turned into another man?"

His breath caught momentarily in his throat.

"Yes. Yes, ma'am, I have."

He asked her why she believed a *birth turning* had occurred, and she described how, over a month ago, she had been gathering berries down by a stand of willows along Lake Nahollo. When her straw hat had blown off and landed in the water, she had scrambled for it, only to be confronted by a cottonmouth moccasin, a mother protecting her brood. The snake, hissing, mouth wide open and white as a full moon, had come at her aggressively.

"I felt my child *turn* within an hour," she said.

Harmony knew the rest. The prevailing swamp superstition held that a pregnant woman, having undergone a horrific fright, would give birth to a deformed child. In many cases, the family of the woman would poison the child while it was still in the womb. Often, as well, the mother-to-be would commit suicide.

"You want me to touch you and see what's there?"

"Yes, sir."

He started to add that he did not embrace the superstition, but he knew that his belief made no difference.

"Would you like for Miss Chosen to be here when I do it?"

She shook her head.

"It don't matter none."

Slowly, then, as if he were engaging in some holy ritual, Harmony lowered himself to one knee and reached out his right hand letting it hover a few inches above the young woman's stomach. He closed his eyes. Layers of darkness like a roiling of storm clouds flooded his thoughts. Images from a bad horror movie he had seen years ago commanded the moment— an imaginary thing of fangs with eyes bloodied and predatory leaped to meet his hand.

But when he pulled it back, something odd took place: the young woman pulled at his hand sharply and pressed it hard onto her stomach, and a dark swirl of vision rocked Harmony forward. He saw the child. Not a human child. A face more like that of a chimpanzee.

"I'm sorry," he cried out. "My God, I'm sorry."

But the young woman would not allow him to remove his hand. If anything she pressed it against her even more forcefully. And she began to repeat herself in a toneless litany.

Turn for me, turn for me, turn for me in that darkness.

Seconds passed like the ticking of eternity.

Out of space and out of time, something finally released. Harmony felt it in his fingertips in contact with the young woman's soft, cotton dress. He felt and saw a morphing in the womb. It was breathtaking.

The young woman began to moan as if giving birth.

Harmony's other leg gave way, and he fell to both knees as if in supplication.

"Turn," he whispered.

The young woman trembled.

Harmony once again saw inside the womb. And he was astonished.

Nearly a minute more fled away.

He could hear the young woman's teeth chattering.

Then he heard her say, "You gone tell what you see?"

"It's there," he said.

"What's it be?"

"A thing like a miracle."

"Not gone need killin'? My boy not a monster? Am *I* not gone need to kill my own self?"

"No."

"What about it all? Can't you say, sir?"

He nodded. He forced a smile.

"You be carryin' a normal child. A girl baby. Gone be a pretty one, I believe."

And he bit his tongue to keep from falling away in a dead faint.

"What happened down there?" said Chosen.

"A mystery within a mystery."

"You're bein' *called* with a loud voice. Do you see that now?"

Harmony nodded. "I know that's right." He swallowed with difficulty. "Full on, it was like a force working through me—seemed to come di-rectly from that young woman."

"She needed you."

He climbed into his boat. He felt physically weakened, spiritually emboldened.

"Say 'hey' to Maybelline for me," said Chosen.

"She's close to droppin' her coonies."

Suddenly she grabbed and embraced him with a strength that surprised him.

"Come around again when you can," she said.

"I'll do that. Thank you for … all of everything."

He pushed off in his boat.

"Promise you'll come again?"

In the bright wash of swamp sun, he tipped his hat in the affirmative.

And she turned away quickly so that he could not see the welling of her tears.

BROTHER HARMONY
AND THE MIDNIGHT WOMAN

H is eyes kept growing back.

Harmony, shirtless, quietly celebrated having spent two days nailing a new, tarpaper covering for the roof of his shack. Evening stood aside to let sundown parade amazing colors. There was no breeze. The Gresham brothers had delivered precious cargo—several jars of what they claimed might just be their strongest summer brew yet. They dubbed it, "Panther Water," and to Harmony's system, it did appear to have claws that tore at one's tongue and ceased not with a rage down one's throat and into one's stomach and, as the eventual target, one's liver.

He toasted the skill and wickedness of the Gresham brothers.

His eyes kept growing back.

"Well, shit if I know where the fuck that's coming from?" he softly muttered to himself. Words they were that troubled the endless reverie of a man who had begun to feel good 'n fine about being prompted to his former calling. Those words broke in upon unpredictable moments in a voice he normally heard when a visitor was on the way—a proleptic indicator without fail.

He glanced around.

Maybelline had apparently headed off into the swamp to squeeze out her coonies. Would she return? Or would she rebirth herself in the wild and become a permanent denizen? Hard to say.

He waited for twilight to steal most the energy of the day,

and then he went inside, put back on his usual outfit, and settled in to listen to music and to think about Chosen and, for rea-
sons thorny and mysterious, about Sway de Rille as well. Two
vastly different women. How could a man be attracted to both
of them? He loved Chosen. No question there. Sway? Well, he
was pretty certain he didn't love her; he admitted, however, that
he clearly *lusted* after her. So there it was. The naked truth, so
to speak.

His eyes kept growing back.

"Oh, Lord baby Jesus, what's that comin' from?"

His head began to ache.

Gritting his teeth, he pressed a CD into his player, unscrewed
another Mason jar of "Panther Water," and turned up the volume of "Bony Moronie" by Larry Williams. The rip and thrum
of the sax, the plangent, eagerly meaningful tone of a great,
black singer from the 50s.

I got a girl named Bony Moronie
She's as skinny as a stick of macaroni
But I love her, she loves me....

Harmony sang along, smiled, and when he belched, a tiny
dragon of fire climbed up from his nether regions into his throat.
His eyes watered. His nose burned. Williams was amazing.
And, once, in fact, Harmony had received a visit from the spirit
of the supremely talented man who had died from an apparent
gunshot wound to the head, but the spirit had *seemed* to say
that the truth might not be known. Could there have been foul
play? The incident left Harmony in wonderment and despair
for several days.

When the tracks of Williams spun to an end, Harmony
closed his eyes.

Something told him to listen to the approach of darkness.

Yes, more music, this time coming from the far end of the
shack.

Sister Chaos was playing jazz. Not just *any* jazz.

She was playing The Bird. Charlie Parker.

Twelve-bar blues—Bird Changes.

A recording of "Bloomdido" with Parker on sax and Dizzy Gillespie on trumpet.

The music swam at Harmony. His headache drained away like dishwater.

Then another piece: "Blues for Alice"—music you could dance to in the dark, drink to after midnight, with screaming tones somehow tender and mellow. The genius of Parker blowing on a hard reed. Listening to this music, you could believe in the phenomenon of starry sorcery.

Suddenly clear headed and lucid, Harmony asked himself a question: *Are terrific and terrible choices left to us?* Something he'd read somewhere long ago offered a deflective answer: *fly on, fly on, fly on, fly on, and let happen what will happen....* He decided to see whether Sister Chaos, a woman married to solitude, might be amenable to conversation, though mainly he wanted to recount his success with the young mother-to-be at Chosen's. But when he reached her door, the healing jazz faded into the night, and as he leaned down to the keyhole, he froze.

Just above the doorknob was the bloody outline of a small hand.

She came in the fierce heat of the following afternoon.

Sway de Rille poling. Lilith, the big cat, seated regally in the prow.

And a passenger Harmony almost overlooked.

"Brother Harmonica, are you ta home?"

Stepping out into the scorching air, he watched the mesmerizing manner in which her body moved like that of a cobra—it *swayed*. And he chuckled to himself at the lousy pun.

"My name is not _____."

"Hey," she interrupted, "I brung you a troubled heart. I'm thinkin' you know her."

He did, indeed.

A thin, black, middle-aged woman named "Jamesia," attendant to Sister Georgia. Annoyed, Lilith shifted lazily out of the way so that Harmony could help the woman on shore.

Sway de Rille blew him a kiss and poled away grinning lasciviously.

Still annoyed, Lilith swished her tail with that pissed off, back and forth jerky motion that all cats apparently have in their DNA.

"Welcome, Miss Jamesia. Guess you're not just visitin'. You got darkness? Who sent you?"

The frail woman raised her eyes to him as if she'd given up hope.

"Crow Speak," she said.

Once inside, he took her immediately to his area behind the curtain. He lit a candle and invited her to sit. He removed his top hat and looked at her closely. Her attention appeared to be glued to one of his signs, the one reading, *Love Is as Strong as Spirit, as Hard as Hell.* Hers was the face of a whisperer, a listener, or one who waits for what she fears will arrive, uninvited, to the door of her life. She wore a white, pillbox hat and matching white, crown veil and a string of cheap pearls. In such attire, she looked as if she might be attending a funeral. A small, white hanky had been pinned over the upper left hand side of her solid blue dress. He assumed that the heart beneath that hanky was as tiny as that of an old dwarf.

However, she possessed glittery eyes, cold and yet fiery. They told him that she desperately needed *something*. She sat before him like a frightened child, one unable to tell the difference between the word *fire* and an actual flame. Harmony was puzzled. So he stalled. He asked about Sister Georgia. In turn, Jamesia informed him that the ancient woman was holding her own.

"My cousin, Quinella, gone be sittin' with her while's I'm here."

Harmony sighed.

Curiously enough, it seemed that being with this woman caused time to slow like rain when it is about to stop.

"Is 'Crow Speak' your spirit guide? A Cherokee spirit guide, I'd suppose."

"Yessir."

"Why doesn't that guide address your issue?"

"Because he has fears to do so."

"I see. Well, back on up and say what it is you need."

It took her a good while.

As a *midnight woman*—that is, a midwife to both whites and blacks—she had *caught* her share of abnormal babies. None, though, quite like one some twenty years back, a boy child named "William" or, to most, "Sweet William," whose mother died giving birth to him.

"Most blood in a birthin' I done ever seed," Jamesia explained.

"What of exceptional strangeness marked him?"

"His eyes."

"Crossed?"

"No, sir. Every day or so they would die—like berries on a bush. Dry up and fall out. Then—why, his eyes kept growing back again."

Harmony's heart beat loudly in his throat.

"That the truth, ma'am?"

"It be, sir."

"What else?"

"As a little wee one, not walkin' long, he took on *away*. He did, sir."

Harmony rocked back and studied her. He knew her reference. *Away*. It meant that the child had come under the power of swamp fairies. The *forgetful people*, as they were called. Those treacherous folk who, he'd been told, resided in the Next Dimension of the Multiverse or, possibly, in a parallel Nahollo Swamp, or, at the least, on another astral plane.

"I must tell you, Miss Jamesia, that I do *not* believe in such. But go on with your tale."

"Like as one *away*, Sweet William went about his days in a dream, sometimes stayin' in bed all day. He'd roam at night. No one could tend him. He talked too freely to the enchanted ones. Well, and then one day when he was five or maybe six, he got the *touch*, a sudden pain and a horrible swelling on his stomach where they'd put their fingers."

"So he went then into transition?"

"He did. Before that, though, I saw with my own eyes how he could change size, and I was there when he came to me and tried to speak and save himself, but his tongue was like a stone."

"Why did the fairies want him?"

"For years ahead. For a time when he could become the husband of one of them."

"Has he come to you in spirit?"

"Yessir."

"With a message? With a task?"

She nodded, but her face fell. She began, quietly, sedately, to sob into her hanky. And then, leaning forward, Harmony noticed something on her cheek. A scar. Alive it seemed to be—as if it were animated with a malicious snake-like existence of its own.

"But," he said, "I gather you can't decipher his message. That you want me to be the go between."

She choked into another nod.

"Let me have your hand, Miss Jamesia."

She gave it to him and shuddered.

He closed his eyes and raised his left hand to his forehead. He petitioned the spirit of Sweet William. After nearly a minute, the connection was made. A high-pitched voice twittered behind Harmony's right ear. It was the implacable tone of one needing help—needing help for someone else. Harmony listened. And when the spirit had delivered his spiel, Harmony said to Jamesia,

"He needs your talent as a midnight woman."

"Why me, sir? There be other midwives."

Harmony shrugged and shook his head.

"He needs you now. He was insistent. And … he asks that I accompany you."

"But will you?"

"I think that I should."

So they began.

He held both of her hands and blew out the candle He told her to relax, empty her mind. He told her that they would soon, together, enter a hypnagogic state, somewhere between sleeping and waking.

"Don't be frightened by the vibration."

Their bodies hummed for the better part of a minute.

"Now the lifting. Just let go."

He heard her issue a soft gasp as their physical selves fell away.

"Don't look back at your body. Don't look back."

At first they encountered an extraordinary quietness. Then space and time contracted. A horrible little silence held sway. Harmony continued to grip the spiritual essence of her hand as they entered a shadowy area unlike any other astral place he had ever experienced. Something precious and yet unholy about it.

They drifted into a vast, malignant determination, a somewhere beyond.

Ab-human presences watched as they were pulled towards what Harmony assumed was the *locus* of Sweet William and the one who needed Jamesia's aid. Shadows moved in incomprehensible ways. Up ahead, two figures wavered in a meager light.

Harmony suddenly stopped. He thought he'd heard someone call his name.

Jamesia, trembling, continued on.

Harmony felt a lightning bolt of hope strike at the core of his human essence.

"Aidan!" he called out. "Aidan, is it you?"

No response.

"Marlena? Lena, my Lena, are you there?"

No, he knew his wife wouldn't likely be. The astral plane probably did not admit suicides. And yet this was the plane of the forgetful people. Perhaps....

Then panic.

He rushed ahead, knowing he should not have let Jamesia go on alone. He saw the three of them enclosed in a deliberate force that made them barely discernible. Sweet William turned to greet him; the young man's eyes were dead, the sockets momentarily empty before new whites and pupils blossomed eerily there. It seemed the intention of the shadows was to generate darkness even though the tenor of the scene he observed took on a preternatural calm.

Jamesia lowered herself to a spread of straw where a young fairy woman writhed in pain. Sweet William shrank in size to hover close to her. With every fiber of his essence, Harmony sensed that an unimaginable birthing was about to occur. He levitated there and waited.

The moment was full and hungry and intensely silent.

Until the screams shattered the shadows as if they were panes of glass.

It was Jamesia screaming.

The young fairy woman reached a hand out to her.

Darkness fell like an angry clap of thunder.

Harmony pulled Jamesia towards him, and they released themselves, a snapping back to their near and far away bodies. As he did so, it was there, smoldering in the air: the immeasurable rage of Sweet William.

Returning to Harmony's shack, they recovered very slowly. The night bore them on. Just before dawn, Harmony fired up his lantern. Crushed and crumpled and beyond tears, Jamesia sat on a cypress chair and quaked.

How had it ended?

Harmony watched her and felt helpless to console the woman. Had she lacked the courage to help the young fairy woman? Certainly, one needed courage to exist in the world of spirit.

Or was it something else?

Had it been Jamesia's choice not to bring another fairy creature into the astral plane? Such a creature might have, in turn, broken through to the realm of humans and wreaked all sorts of havoc.

Harmony felt bewildered and frightened.

Again he noticed the scar on Jamesia's cheek.

Then one thing more: on the other cheek a small, bloody handprint.

BROTHER HARMONY
AND A CELLO OF THE UNKNOWN

Jamesia went down the road to madness and forgot the way back to sanity. Brother Harmony checked on her once, but she did not appear to recognize him. To get some distance, physically and emotionally, from the nerve-jangling events that he experienced on the astral plane, he turned the shack over to Sister Chaos for nearly a week, donned his work clothes and hiked in to Sweet River where he took on again the identity of Alan Wayne Trapman; he joined a construction crew building new student housing on the campus of Mantis College. It was hard, honest, sweaty, dusty work. Harmony (or Trapman) was a skilled carpenter. But after three days, he began to long for the wet, decaying, nose-punching stench of all things dead and dying in Nahollo Swamp. He missed Wasp Heart Bayou. He told himself that he actually missed being Brother Harmony.

He wondered whether any lost souls had come to his shack to be found.

So it was with a pinch of joy that one sultry twilight he returned to his other life, to another world, to the place and to the self he belonged to.

Maybelline was there waiting.

With three coonies that followed her like shadowy globs on tiny paws.

Harmony held and cuddled them; Maybelline looked on proudly.

"You're welcome—you and yours—to stay," he told her.

But when dawn arrived much too quietly, she and her

keep-close-to-Mama coonies had gone into the wild, and he knew that she would not likely ever again entertain domesticity. Under his breath, in his best imitation of Chuck Berry, Harmony crooned,

Oh, Maybelline, why can't you be true?
You done started off doin' the things you used to do.

He fixed a pot of coffee and a batch of grits and whispered to himself, "May the gods of Nahollo watch over you, Mama Maybelline, and creatures like you."

Then he went to the door of Sister Chaos and informed her of his presence.

Her silence was tumultuous.

Then he noticed something.

His breath caught: the small, bloody handprint had disappeared.

His thoughts flashed to Jamesia, but he was too weary to hold and ponder them.

He napped until around noon. Ate two slices of watermelon.

He sat outside and stared into a realm that still remembered *Genesis* and perhaps even the dinosaurs. He thought he knew a good many words in the vocabulary of the old swamp—its vowels were water, its consonants were fear. The harsh, hot light of the steamy place preached tenderness, but did not practice it. At night, that same swamp was a satisfied god falling asleep.

On his steps, Harmony mused.

Before, that is, he began to hear, in a pleasant rise and flow of sound, music drifting in on mirages of humidity.

Cello music.

Could that possibly be?

From whence?

Of numerous things he could not be certain.

Yet, this: it was the music of Bach.

Inside his shack, he waited for what wanted to come. He did not have to wait long.

Though he heard no knock, he opened his door minutes

later to find a lovely, black-haired woman with dark features wearing gypsy clothing—a bright red peasant blouse and a colorful, twirl skirt and the throwback phenomenon of petticoats, layers of them. A cello leaned against the woman like a second self.

Harmony's headache blazed as if set off by anxiety.

Though almost beautiful, the woman looked as if happiness had stepped out of her life and had decided never to return. She seemed a widow who was becoming ever more widowed.

"What do you ask?" he said.

The mode of her response unnerved him.

That you listen.

It had been years since anyone had spoken telepathically into his mind. She was skilled at it.

"What is your name?" he said.

She hesitated and lovingly caressed the bridge of the cello. She kissed the strings and then looked up at him.

Zoranza.

He smiled broadly at the obvious phoniness of the name. There was no choice but to invite her in.

Behind the curtain of his inner sanctum, in the candlelight, she looked nearly as ravishing as his memory of the actress, Gina Lollobrigida, in her role as "Esmeralda" in *The Hunchback of Notre Dame.* The loops of her gold-plated earrings glimmered in their seduction of the light. Her lips were pouty and coated with a hungry, red lipstick. She sat and clutched at the cello protectively.

"Please make yourself comfortable," he said.

She had arrived trailing the earthy aroma of transformation. It was as if her life resisted being made into story. She eyed him as if she feared he was *not* the one she needed.

Will you listen to my playing?

"Yes," he said, "and I shall try to comply with whatever else you request of me."

She hesitated.

When I have finished playing, do not be shocked or repulsed by what happens next.

"What are you asking?"

That you free me from this strange flame of obsession.

When he started to respond, she raised her bow as if to signal that the time for words must end, the time for music must begin. Methodically, precisely, she sat towards the front of the chair, her bare, left foot slightly forward. The cello appeared to rest gently against her full breasts and was balanced between her knees. She employed no endpin stop. The neck and scroll of the instrument seemed to hover to the left of her head and angled slightly to the right. Her left hand readied itself for vibrato; her right hand held the bow with no tension—with it she would stroke the strings intimately.

She hissed into his mind in a sensual whisper.

Bach's Cello Suite No. 5. The one known as "Darkness." I will play the Sarabande.

As she edged to the cusp of playing, Harmony studied her as if suddenly seeing her for the first time: she existed there before him, nameless, anonymous, a parable, a thing made of longing. Longing for what? *To be freed,* she had said. She burned there, solitary and luminous. Did she have friends? Family? Attachments? Lovers? He strangely assumed not. An axiom from the past flooded his thoughts: *She who plays beautiful music is whole and complete.* But perhaps that was far from the truth.

Bow met strings.

And then Harmony truly saw. Her music alone spoke to her. Did it take her too far? Cello music shaped her beauty. As she played, he found it difficult to look at her eyes; he did not want, by chance, to meet her gaze. Being this close to her and to the music of Bach carried him into a space of intense listening. He entered not the spirit of the moment, but rather the spirit of his own depths. Once, during the first thirty seconds, he sensed that she was searching for eternity in his face.

The music.

Great beauty in the somberness. The dying of the day and of the year. Dark tones, yet peaceful, serious, sad. Music that connected him with the feeling of reading a sad novel. For over three minutes, the Sarabande captured and obliterated time. It spoke of the truly mysterious. It was stark, minimal, severe, lovely, simple. And devastating. Painfully pleasurable to experience.

The music shaped itself in a single breath.

It matched the beating of his heart. It assumed an eternal flow in its moment-to-moment futurity. It juxtaposed life and eternity. The more deeply Harmony listened, the more he became conscious that his breathing was in sync with the pace of the playing, the twists and the turns.

"How beautiful," he murmured, then realized that his head-ache had relented.

The melodic line was endless.

And then something more.

The telepathic in a new register: Zoranza's emotions and subconscious sensations had become *his* as well. The phenomenon startled him. It was as if she were hurling herself at him, a flame upstriking in her performance body, one that she could not extinguish. Harmony was surrendering to the reverie of being so close to the admixture of her pleasure and her terror. He shut his eyes and imagined that there was not enough sun for her dreams to ripen. He imagined that her life might once have been rare and shy and white—like that of a unicorn.

But now.

The cello was her cage.

She had been captured.

He imagined her voice, the vocalization behind the telepathy, her words. He *felt* them more than he *heard* them. She was speaking: *I want to begin life without this.*

Harmony to himself: *What am I entering?*

Zoranza's playing was purely unpremeditated.

Trust what is difficult, he told himself.

And then it was over.

And then a something else began.

Except that when it was over, he could not recall a beginning beyond his desire to reach out and touch the cello, this unknown thing that had abducted its player. Perhaps she had shrieked.

The scene unfolded like a reel of pornography, a murky, inaccessible foregrounding of bodies: Zoranza and the cello, with the woman planting kisses that blossomed on the surface of the instrument, the red outline of lips sensuous, her fingers fondling strings and pressing up and down, back and forth.

Though surprised—a touch shocked—Harmony could not keep from chuckling.

What the fuck?

"Jesus," he murmured.

Her moans and groans escalated quickly. After she removed every stitch of her clothing, she pulled the cello down upon her and straddled it and bucked against it, sending out discordant strains of sound.

He wanted to shout, "Stop this!"

But was too mesmerized to do so.

Then, after wrestling herself atop her partner, she took her bow in hand and swished it. Her naked body was stunning, the breasts nearly perfect.

Harmony stepped back.

He hated that he was smiling. More so, that he was aroused.

Cries of anticipated pleasure rode out of her as she pressed up from the cello, giving herself space to insert the bow between her legs. The seconds flickered, and as Harmony took in the scene he was intensely aware of her hunger for this alien soul, this surrogate for sexual need. This macabre masturbation.

This obsession.

By the time she issued her final utterances of bliss, her surrender to the demands of her orgasm, Harmony was nearly exhausted through his voyeurism. Instinctively, he reached to snuff out the candle between two fingers. He was breathing heavily. He felt foolish.

Yet, he laughed nervously.

He could think of absolutely nothing to say.

In the aftermath breathing of both of them, she spoke into his thoughts.

Help me.

The words of someone calling up from a bizarre darkness.

Fumbling about, he re-lit the candle.

"Put on your clothes and stay right here. I'll return momentarily."

At the door to the room of Sister Chaos, he felt much too dizzy to speak. He blinked, and he wiped sweat from his brow and fanned himself with his top hat. He fought another urge to chuckle.

He stared at the door and received an answer to his unspoken question.

It burst into flames.

Not real flames, of course, but those connecting the imaginations of him and Sister Chaos.

The conflagration lasted only a matter of seconds.

Harmony whispered, "Thank you," and returned to his patron.

Twilight neared as he led her and her cello less than a hundred yards from his shack to a clearing of ground with little danger of losing control of a burn. It took less than a half an hour to build a pyre of dry limbs, a piling of oak and pine and dogwood and poplar.

When he took the cello and bow from her, he said, "I believe it has to be this way."

Her eyes downcast, she said nothing, perhaps nodded ever so slightly.

Harmony reverently placed the cello and bow atop the wood.

He made the woman stand at a distance as he stuffed gasoline soaked rags among the gathering of limbs and dropped a match onto the configuration. It's possible that he heard her stifle a shriek. Of protest? Of relief?

The eager flames found wings.

Harmony looked on, his headache returning.

The blaze shaped a pyramid, releasing sparks and smoke.

At first, the cello received the fire without protest, with the muteness of an inanimate object rather than the resignation of a lover.

But then the wonder of the smoke struck Harmony full force.

As it coiled and spiraled upward, it seemed to send out the gloriously dark strains of Bach, his magnificent Cello Suite No. 5.

For several moments, the music paralyzed Harmony.

In the distance, he heard an owl cry out, then the response of another.

And he could move again. And speak.

"This is what we had to do," he said.

When he turned to see her reaction, she had disappeared. Vanished.

Only her clothing remained behind.

Naturally enough, Harmony searched about for her, until he felt her inside his head, murmuring something indecipherable, though he believed—or wanted to believe—that she had escaped into a supra-sensible realm, into a silence that music leaves behind.

Something she had been seeking.

Something that had been seeking her.

For another hour or so, the music of Bach drifted out into the swamp, spreading in a soft blanket before darkness claimed it as its own.

BROTHER HARMONY, DOG HOBBLE AND THE GRABBLE MAN

For several ensuing nights there was a roaring in the wind that chased Bach from the swamp. Heavy rain pounded Wasp Heart Bayou. Ashes upon wet ashes mounded where the cello of the unknown was executed. When the rains ceased, Brother Harmony spent several more days looking for Zoranza (or whoever she truly was), but he found no trace of her, not even footprints. He decided to donate her clothing to Chosen's charity collection.

He would tell the woman he loved about the cello obsession.

About Zoranza, the woman tongued with Bach.

Naked in the somewhere. Her beauty grew each time Harmony imagined her, though he would not mention that to Chosen.

Wherever Zoranza was, he told himself that it must be a realm beyond the language of the living; wherever she was, she had been freed of her dilemma. Perhaps once again she would vocalize words, words that Harmony had never thought to speak.

She had been redeemed from fire by fire.

Isn't that how we live? he reasoned to himself, *To be consumed by one fire or another?*

Of course, he related the tableau to Sister Chaos.

As always, she responded in the language of silence.

Then one morning Harmony woke thinking about an old friend.

Dog Hobble.

He needs me.

Having learned over the years not to reject the voice of the daemonic, Harmony rolled out of bed, brewed coffee and concentrated—*Is my friend in trouble?*

Darlington "Dog" Hobble, who had roamed Nahollo Swamp with him before and throughout their teenage years, was most decidedly *not* the type of man who needed help from anyone else. He was tall, blond, muscular, almost always clad in overalls, no shirt beneath, and wore serious hunting boots. Hatless and tan, he lived alone and embraced a single goal: to exist without pain and boredom. Skilled at both hunting and fishing, he was as self-sufficient as a denizen of the great swamp could be.

But Harmony knew this about him: the man was haunted.

He needs me.

Case closed.

Loading his boat with a few necessities, Harmony struck out, not even bothering to share his plans with Sister Chaos.

"Conjure man, I'm tellin' you that her eyes are wild."

Dog Hobble spoke with a distant, faraway look, yet with a smile and with a tone suggesting that the reality behind his observation thrilled him.

It had taken Harmony most of the morning to reach Dog's abode, a refurbished houseboat in backwaters so shallow that the man had to wait for heavy rains to move it, should he desire to do so. As was customary, when Harmony had come within a hundred yards of where he thought Dog must be, he pitched back and released a skunk ape howl before stopping at the largest cypress handy and banging a sturdy branch against it in a trio of tree knocks. He waited dutifully for Dog to return the howl and the knocks—which he did. Not that either man believed in the legendary swamp creature sometimes known as "The Booger Man," but they both knew an old and slightly lunatic swamper—a hermit by the name of James Joseph Gresham—who claimed that as a young man he shot one of the mythical apes and ate it. Insisted that it tasted a little like wild boar.

Perched on stools, the two men slipped easily into the habitual role of old friends. As usual, Harmony noticed the horrific scar forking down from Dog's right shoulder, over the bicep to the elbow area; it evidenced runic symbols of a gator attack that occurred when Dog was just fifteen.

"Saw your bunk mate t'other day," Dog began.

"This is a hell of a long way from our shack for Sister Chaos to be," said Harmony. "You sure that's who you saw?"

Raising his right hand as if he were about to swear in a court of law, Dog smiled, then bucked up seriously.

"Conjure man, I saw her. I heard her not more 'n two nights ago. She sings the swamp is what I'm knowin'."

"I couldn't say," said Harmony. "She's never nothing but a mystery to my way of reading."

Dog was adamant.

"She sings me not to fear. The night takes suck of her, conjure man, and she to it."

"Be careful, friend, likely she's lookin' for somethin' no one else would want to find."

The only soul on earth who ever called him "conjure man" was Dog. He wasn't being derogatory, it was simply a matter of never being fully comfortable calling him "Brother Harmony" or "Trapman."

"Hey, like I said, she sings me not to fear."

"She does, does she?"

Dog shrugged. He clutched one of the half dozen jars of "Panther Water" Harmony had brought, unscrewed it and drank down three fingers of it before softly shrieking his approval of the brew and pretending that he'd just swallowed liquid barbed wire. He studied the contents of the jar as if to see whether some alien creature swam around in it. Like a piranha or an electric eel.

"So, tell me, you bein' the ghost and ghoul man—what you sayin' we *should ought* to be afraid of?"

Before Harmony could dredge up a response, he found himself hit by a wave of sadness. It puzzled him. He half wished he hadn't come. Dejection swarmed around him like a ball of mosquitoes. He wrote it off as possibly discomfort in the face of hearing Dog speak of Sister Chaos. But why that?

"Afraid of? Same thing as ever—the heedless ones among us."

"Because they wanna kill us?"

"No, because they have no fuckin' idea *what* they want. That's what's spooky."

Dog laughed with his whole body.

"Shit, I don't doubt that. I don't." His laughter trailed away gradually. He looked out into the heat of the day, the manner in which it spread like something substantial across duckweed slavered over the swamp water. He sighed, and as he did so he appeared to bring up a bucket of abject sobriety from a deep well within him. "You know what I've learned, conjure man?" And he nodded mechanically before completing his declaration. "That the living haunt themselves. They sure as hell do. *Relentlessly.*"

Then he returned to his jar of moonshine.

Harmony had only rarely heard his friend express himself that way. Had *never* heard him utter a word such as *relentlessly.*

"Dog," he said, "I came to see you because I got a strong sense you had a need for me." When his friend wouldn't meet his eyes, he continued, cautiously. "Tell me the God honest truth—you been seein' the ghost of 'Faithful'?"

There is something huge and dark in Nahollo Swamp that can claw and bite through the defenses of any and every man and woman. Brother Harmony and Dog Hobble had faced that reality many times. More so, they knew the swamp well enough not to try to change it and, least of all, to try to tame it. The best one could do was not inflict too much pain upon another and to accept the indifference and mystery of nature and the whispery possibility that the supernatural was part and parcel of that same, reigning nature.

So the afternoon flowed towards twilight. Each killed a jar of hooch, and Dog avoided responding to Harmony's question until he apparently decided his visitor and old friend had tapped into something beyond the pale.

"Conjure man, let me ask you something: What is it you're really tryin' to do with this spiritualism thing? You know, talkin' to the departed an' such like?"

Harmony nodded as if to indicate it was a fair question.

"Well, sir, ... guess you could say I'm hopin' to alleviate those who're sufferin' and to understand those who're damned."

A touch shaky on his feet, Dog pushed up from his stool and jabbed his thumb into his chest.

"I'm both of 'em. I'm *sufferin'* and I'm *damned*."

Harmony paused to connect with his friend's level of seriousness.

"How bad is it?" he said.

Dog shook his head and pointed at his left eye.

"This come on 'cause I've been thinkin' night an' day 'bout Faithful."

Harmony had earlier noticed the cataract, the crystalline whiteness of it as if the eye were inhabited by frost.

"I don't connect cause and effect here," he said.

"Me neither," said Dog. "Not so's it makes sense. Just seems like she's callin' to me. That maybe if I could see her—her ghost or whatever—then I could ... fuck, I don't know."

"You want me to try to contact her?"

"No. No, not that." He wiped at his lips and looked almost too miserable for words. "But if there's any healin' in you, maybe you could give sight back to this one bad eye."

"I'll give it my best shot, Dog. You know I will."

A finished silence claimed them. They drank quietly, drank as if preparing for something awkward or embarrassing, something requiring courage. After nearly a minute into that silence, the flight of a blue heron caught Dog's attention.

"It's always been Faithful. I can't see it never changin'."

"You loved her. You *loved* her. Strong as a love could be," said Harmony.

"Shit, though—it brought me to killin' a man. Don't forget that."

Falling into memory, Harmony recalled how the girl, Faithful, barely fifteen, had registered in the book of Dog's lust just on the other side of his turning eighteen. He was gone on her, and, so it seemed, she on him. But she belonged to the Haggardy cult of The House of the Rising Dead who reserved the right—so they believed—to choose a husband for her, which they did: an itinerant, revivalist preacher known as Terence Flintock, a shag of a man. When Faithful, a good friend to

Chosen, was delivered the news regarding her marriage, she lit out into the swamp. Flintock pursued her.

And events closed down in a black silence.

Flintock claimed that when he found her, she had drowned herself. Dog, assessing the situation from the outside, read it differently. On the night following Faithful's burial, Dog ambushed Flintock; they fought each other like demons from the crack of doom. Dog won the fight. Smashed in Flintock's face so badly that grown men vomited at the sight of it. Dog beat the man to death. Received a manslaughter sentence and served nine years in prison. Harmony visited him at least once a month. So did Chosen.

So did the ghost of Faithful.

"Dog," said Harmony, "allow me if you will to put my touch on that wintry eye of yourn."

"You can heal it?"

"We'll see."

Pressing the fingers of his left hand down firmly on Dog's eye, Harmony lowered his head in concentration and in prayer to the deepest, oldest part of himself. Dog quivered and quaked. For the better part of five minutes, Harmony held the pressure; he relented only when his fingers tired, at which point he said, "That's gone have to do it. I poured out as much healin' as I have."

Dog blinked, then blinked some more.

Harmony leaned in close to the eye.

"Damn it all to hell," he muttered. "I'm sorry, friend, it just didn't take."

Disappointed, yet resigned to the results, Dog cupped a hand on to Harmony's shoulder.

"Don't get down in the mouth, conjure man. I'm just too much of a sorry, God damned bastard for healin' to come my way. Shit, it's all fine 'n good."

"No, it is not," said Harmony. "Not one damn bit."

They skipped supper as twilight stalked them. They drank, and then they drank some more until both gently passed out, having obliterated the entire cache of Panther Water. First light, they eventually woke, splitting headaches and one thing more:

Nahollo clap. The cause of said affliction was some faulty ingre-
dient in the alcohol they'd consumed; the manifestation of the
affliction was the most painful urination ever experienced by
man or beast.

"Like pissin' fish hooks an' razor blades," was how Dog
described it.

In the thralls of a monster hangover, they somehow brewed
coffee, shoe-leather-strong coffee, drank four or five cups after
which Harmony heard himself declare, "I've got the answer.
We're gone to find the 'Grabble Man.'"

Dog's chest heaved. He glanced at his sobering friend in
response.

"Shit, no, we's not. No way in hell. No, no, no."

Harmony rubbed his cheeks hard and blubbered his lips.

"You know the old superstition. Maybe there's some truth
in it. Worth a try."

Dog protested. Then they slept close to noon. Ate cold biscuits and cold, fried catfish and drank more coffee. Finally, Dog
gave in.

"But I'm sure as hell not dancin' a jig 'bout this, conjure
man. You know my history with that fella."

"I do, sir," said Harmony. "I do."

They lit out mid-afternoon, toting pine tar sticks for torches
later on should they not return before dark. Of course,
Harmony had heard Dog's account of the long ago gator attack
many times, but Dog honored him with still another telling. Of
being smack in the area they were traversing and of sighting
the Grabble Man—"grabble" a swamp term meaning to dig or
scratch at the earth. That's how the Grabble Man, whose real
name and origination were unknown, survived by clawing up
roots of all kind and by catching frogs, turtles, crayfish and
such like. He didn't go hungry. Over the years a superstition
grew up around this peculiar man—that a "sighting" of him
brought salubrious results health wise—in other words, just
seeing the man could heal what ailed one.

"It was a blister hot day, an' I was dippin' in a pool of backwater close about here, an' I spied him. And then he spied me.

The Grabble Man. Gray-white beard like Spanish moss that hung down to his belly button. He's wearin' nothin' but a loin-cloth, I guess you call it. There was a somethin' given 'bout him, you know?"

Harmony intruded.

"But how can be sure he brought on the gator to attack you?"

"Well, sir, I could see it in his eyes. He didn't like it that I had sneaked up on 'im unawares."

"Another thing, Dog, how can you be sure he didn't *save* your ass from that gator? Maybe. Maybe he talked that gator out of makin' a snack of your whole arm."

"Shi-i-i-i-t! It wudn't like that, conjure man. I 'bout bled to death. That Grabble Man, he don't like me."

"You don't *know* that."

They trekked on. Harmony hugged a good feeling that the Grabble Man could melt away Dog's cataract. What did they have to lose? Quarter of a mile deeper into a remote area of Nahollo they slowed. A wet, prairie hammock spread out directly in front of them, while a path of sorts wound to their left and rose up to pass under an outcropping of granite. When they veered on to the path, Harmony stopped in his tracks. He glanced over at Dog who smiled weakly.

"Conjure man, you remember me tellin' you 'bout this, don't you?"

Harmony nodded soberly.

Yes, of course, he did. This was the last spot apparently where someone had seen Aidan—seen him alive anyway. Dog had seen him. Over the years Harmony had visited this path recalling Dog describing how the eleven-year-old, long-black-haired boy was running towards the rocks with joy in his stride. Running like boys in their dreams.

Though he knew it was futile, Harmony tried again to use his paranormal abilities to receive a glimpse of his beloved son. Tried hard. But, as usual, nothing came. Just a cold, black, grim nothingness.

"Let's go lo-cate the Grabble Man," he said, finally. "Wasting time here."

Another hour passed before the rough path ended in a very shallow run.

"Where to now?" said Dog. "I'm 'bout ready to head back."

Suddenly Harmony felt it.

A presence.

"We need to wade up this run."

So they did. For another fifty yards. The run flowed down a piece and became a creeklet, and where that creeklet rounded a bend, Harmony looked on ahead as they began to lose the light and the heat of the day.

"Holy shit, Dog, look up there."

Harmony pointed. Still another forty or fifty yards away the creeklet gained speed purling over a bed of rocks. A lone man crouched over the running water; he was clawing assiduously at the mud and the larger stones.

"Jesus, God Almighty," Dog murmured, "it's him."

Though Harmony believed the Grabble Man hadn't yet seen them, he wondered whether he might be able to hear their thoughts. He seemed an apparition. Like something elemental, living on water and air and earth. Like one unwilling to be fed as humans are. Like one who conversed with the moon and the rain and the wind. But not a beggar. No, if anything, the swamp begged from him. Or perhaps his true, sustaining substance was *solitude.*

This was an Earth Man.

One who knew the persistence of being alone. He was the living embodiment of timelessness. His psyche and spirit belonged to Otherness.

Harmony reached for Dog and whispered, "You got to look him full in the face. You understand?"

His breathing ragged, Dog pulled away.

"I can't never do this. All's I feel like is findin' a place to hide."

Harmony's neck flamed in anger.

"God damn it, Dog," he hissed. "We ain't boys no more. The hiding places, they're all gone by."

When they turned in the direction of the Grabble Man, he had disappeared.

Minutes passed.

They fired up their torches, spawning eerie shadows that swallowed up their surroundings. They waded another sixty feet.

"He's never not comin' back," said Dog. "He's done gone to where we can't never follow."

Harmony listened to the twilight.

"No," he muttered. "I'm getting something. I'm hearing it."

"Let's get our asses back home, conjure man."

"No." Harmony was absorbed in listening. A few moments crawled by before he grabbed Dog's wrist. In a voice not at all his, Harmony said, *"You got to seek the wonder of a face you once knew."*

Dog struggled. "What the fuck?" he exclaimed.

And from the shadows the Grabble Man emerged once again.

And he was gesturing for them to follow.

"No!" Dog screamed.

Harmony calmed him.

"Yes. The face, Dog. You've got to seek the face."

"No! He's gone to put us down. We's trespassers."

"Yes," said Harmony, "but you've got to go—I *feel* it, Dog. I *know* it."

And though shaken, they both tracked after the Grabble Man, staying in the creeklet until it emptied in to a dying slough, a large, circular pool of water almost glittering with dead white branches reaching up from the unknown body. The scene danced a macabre, shadow dance.

"Jesus, God!" Dog muttered. "I ain't doin' this."

"Yes. Yes, you are." And he pushed his friend forward.

Even as, once again, the Grabble Man seemed to melt into nothingness.

Dog and Harmony stood at the edge of the slough, the moment totally incomprehensible. Dog stared out into the ugliness of the strange scene.

"What is it?" said Harmony. "What's there?"

"Oh, bless it," said Dog. "I'm seein' this."

But Harmony did not, not at first, until his friend had waded, waist deep out from the shore, wending through small, dead trees towards a gray wash of light. Dog held his pine torch high in his right hand like Lady Liberty. Harmony watched.

And then he gasped.

Up from the slough, just a few yards in front of Dog, a phantom figure rose, the nebulous outline of a person.

He heard Dog call out, "Faithful! Faithful, it's you?"

And it was.

Her hand ghosted out to touch Dog's face.

Harmony heard the man's blissful groan.

A train of seconds passed.

Faithful, a wordless entity, hovered. The night sang out.

Before she sank away, away eternally from the reach of Dog.

When he returned to Harmony's side, he smiled a smile of shock and relief. The frosty eye had thawed. Dog could see clearly. He shivered, and Harmony embraced him, and, for a few seconds at least, the spirit of friendship transformed them into gods and they ruled the dark soul of Nahollo Swamp.

BROTHER HARMONY
AND THE UNSPEAKABLE

Weirdly sculptured torsos of mist barely evaded first rays, and the larger cypresses spread the remnants of night over their naked trunks. Wasp Heart Bayou sank into itself as still as deer at startled gaze. Brother Harmony's love affair with dawn—sunrise tasting the air—showed no signs of abating. The silence shared his pleasure, offering silent impressions in silent spaces. An astonishingly quiet beauty held sway in the furtive and treacherous realm of Nahollo Swamp.

Where did it go—that circumambient darkness from which Harmony stirred? This was the enchanted hour, a moment in time preparing to convulsively transform sentient matter and the psyches of anyone present. Alone, however, Harmony looked on, haunting himself, knowing then that Dog was right, that his friend had wedded inner and outer fears and had been just brave enough to let the ghost of Faithful heal him.

But what about me?

Harmony knew that the phantom ringer in the ghostly tower of *his* introcosm was a young, free spirit who had loved the swamp, had loved to laugh, had loved mysteries and who had been much too friendly with strangers. Aidan. The Kid. Early on, Aidan had clung to his mother; later on, he released himself from her anxieties about his wildness. In her sorrow, Lena found no way to dig herself out of grief, a premature burial more frightening than anything Poe had ever imagined.

She took enough pills to kill three people.

Harmony couldn't save her. And now he still couldn't contact her.

Or Aidan either.

Sun blazing in the east shattered his thoughts. The birds of morning—egrets, herons as well as pine warblers—winged everywhere their primitive, authentic selves demanded. In a few hours, record heat would claim the unthinkable territory of late June. Harmony stood up and went inside; fingering through the walls of his shack, the magical pluckings of jazz guitarists: Sister Chaos was having Johnny Smith's "Walk, Don't Run" for breakfast. By the time Harmony reached her door, Smith had cooled and Wes Montgomery was heating up with "Smokin' at the Half Note." Jazz guitar didn't get any better.

"My buddy, Dog Hobble, says he's been uh seein' you."

Harmony looked down at a pile of true crime magazines Sister Chaos had apparently stacked there to be discarded. Twisting his mouth in distaste, Harmony picked up the copy on top and thumbed into a piece on the "Pig's Ear Killer," a gut-emptying account of a panhandle Florida monster of a fellow who had morphed from eating boiled pig's ear sandwiches to murdering young women, slicing off their tender ears and creating a new kind of sandwich you won't find on the Waffle House menu.

Harmony dropped the disgusting mag and exclaimed, "You ought not to read this godawful shit."

Then he blinked in the shadows.

He stared at the door to his shack mate's room.

Red dots blazed out from a dozen or so spots on the surface.

"Jesus," he whispered.

The dots unsettled him, and so he backed away and returned to his area just in time to see that he had visitors.

Merlin and Mance Gresham.

Harmony hollered them in, shaking hands first with Merlin, the bearded of the two, taller and darker than Mance, who was blond, younger, and who smiled perhaps because Merlin never did. They brought a new batch of refreshment: "Summer Blood," a red, truck stop strong ale, drinkable if you also liked sipping diesel fuel.

"Swamp's gettin' strange," said Mance, grinning.

"Don't I know it," said Harmony as Merlin stared at his top hat as if it were a grotesque growth or some mutant form of turkey vulture that had lit upon Harmony's head.

Taking a folded sheet of paper from a pocket in his overalls, Mance practically stuttered, "We brung this from Chosen. She told us to."

Harmony warmed to images of that woman's flesh before he began to read the following:

Shall thy wonders be known in the dark?
And thy righteousness in the land of forgetfulness?
Alan, love, I need a favor.
—Chosen

The passage was from *Psalms*. Harmony knew, as well, what "the land of forgetfulness" referred to in the context of Nahollo Swamp.

"You boys know what this tis about?"

Merlin looked uncomfortable; so did Mance, and yet he volunteered a cautious response: "Reckon it's them 'Ratchers.'"

Harmony glanced down again at the note.

He sighed.

"Well, shit," he muttered.

"You remember 'Easter'?"

Harmony had to fight to concentrate on Chosen's question, for her beauty, her desirability ushered him far from the kickable reality of the world. He blinked and swallowed and half nodded.

"Real damn weird little girl as I recall. But sweet. Guess she's not *little* no more." He squinted. His voice lost volume. "What's wrong?"

He had lost no time in boating over to see what Chosen needed. Now in her presence and hearing the name of "Easter," he felt a gut punch of unease.

"She's gone need rescuing, I believe."

"What about the rest of her family? I mean, I know the mother and grandfather passed, but the father and the three other children—what is it you aren't saying?"

"Alan, I don't quite know myself, except that the older brother and sister, you see, there's apparently been new tragedies, and you know how these Hardshell folks can be."

Hardshell in Nahollo were Primitive Baptists who stuck to themselves. Old believers in ageless evil and the blood shed on the cross and in the crucifixion of one's heart.

Harmony's tongue ticked dryly. "I suppose I do." He looked away, then back at her. "Was it sickness?"

Chosen's shoulders squirmed. Her face blanched as if painted suddenly with fear.

"No. What we hear is that it's *scunners.*"

Harmony froze.

"You don't mean that."

She pressed her lips together so tightly that it appeared they had dissolved. She trembled. Harmony went to her and held her face against his shoulder.

"Go and help Easter. Please," she said.

Into her hair he said, "There's not somebody from the Hardshell around here that would be better at doin' it?"

"No. They won't. They refuse."

"Why?"

"They're too scared."

He held her for a long time.

The day was losing light rapidly by the time Harmony reached Forgotten Bayou, the homestead of the Ratcher family, the most isolated souls in the whole of the great Nahollo Swamp.

They live in the nowhere, never not, he told himself. *A more wickedly profound solitude can't be imagined.*

Most unnerving of all, Harmony had poled through a stretch of water in which fiery red dots had risen to the surface, their mode threatening—instantly he recalled Sister Chaos, her door.

My God, what's going on?

The dots followed him until the vine-covered hovel of Orlin

Ratcher and his beloveds ghosted into view, then seemed to disappear. Orlin himself, shotgun braced against his shoulder, suddenly stood on the shore as if rooted to the piney woods soil. His long, gray, mossy beard and longish hair fell against his all-black clothes, including a black, slouch hat. The man's eyes were dead. His body wavered unsteadily.

Harmony raised an arm in peaceful salute.

"Mr. Ratcher, sir, I've been told I might could help you. Brother Harmony's the name. You remember me?"

Ratcher's voice was a reedy whistle.

"The spiritualist?"

"Yes, sir. The woman named 'Chosen,' she's been worrying about you and your family."

"She has, has she?" The man gritted his teeth and gripped the shotgun firmly. Anger or something like it flashed across his eyes. "We's done gone past bein' worried on. We's can't live no other way."

"How bad is it, sir?"

Harmony came ashore. Ratcher stared beyond him into a present without a future.

"You armed?"

"No, sir."

Ratcher studied him as if he were something other than human.

"You know *scunners*?" he said.

"Something of them, I do." Harmony paused. "I mean, for most swampers scunners are scoundrels. For Hardshell folks like yourself, they're way more. Something like demons is what I understand."

Ratcher shuddered.

"Like somethin' from outta the mouth of Hell," he said, as if an image of what he and his family had encountered inhabited him and had no intention of leaving.

"You mind if I stay a spell?"

Ratcher shook his head.

"You're welcome to. You found us. Nobody else has even taken a stab at it." But when Harmony offered him a tote bag filled with apples, oranges and homemade bread—gifts from

Chosen—he added, "Can't eat your food. God would punish us for it."

"Your God, though—He's standing by you in your troubles, is He not?"

Growling low in his throat, Ratcher said, "We's too far in sin for that." And having spoken his piece, the man turned and led Harmony to the family hovel, lightless except for a mothy candle in one corner where two forms shifted and chattered to each other, almost chirping like birds. The sounds spoke to the oldest part of Harmony's brain and triggered the irremediable scent of pure terror. The darkness was greasy and stank of soot and bodily odors.

"My chill'drun," said Ratcher. "The boy is 'Micah,' the girl is 'Easter.'"

"Yes, I mostly remember them, especially Easter. Hey, hello."

The boy, dark hair below his shoulders, might have been eight or so; he had the face of a wild dog, eyes too alert and predatory to be human. In his all-black clothing, he was so thin that hunger had abandoned him. But the girl. When Harmony's eyes met hers, he almost had to look away. Her beauty created a ghostly other that appeared to stand beside her, detached, more mature and breathtaking. Her shoulder-length, dark hair feathered so delicately that he wanted to run to her and rub his fingers across it. Her eyes were shiny and golden—the color of a halo. She held the Bible opened in her lap; her fingertips traced down the columns as if she were blind.

Then she startled him, speaking in clear English, her voice older, wiser than her twelve or thirteen years.

"Are you a friend of Miss Chosen?"

Stunned momentarily, Harmony was speechless. He nodded several seconds before he spoke.

"Yes. Yes, I am. She … she reminded me that you stayed with her a couple of years before returning to your family. She's been … concerned about you—about all of you."

"I like your hat," she said, smiling sadly as she deflected his comments.

"Some folks do," he said, removing it out of politeness.

"Makes me look taller and smarter." He returned her smile. Inside his pity, he liked her.

Suddenly at his shoulder, Ratcher wheezed and snuffled before whispering, "You've come to a godforsaken place. You have. We's won't hold it 'gainst you if you turn an' go on back."

"No. No, I'll stay. I might—I'll try to help any way I can."

Ratcher issued a snort of seeming disgust and went back outside. Micah chased after him, howling low like a distressed animal.

Harmony then concentrated on Easter.

"Are you finding answers there?" he said, pointing to the opened Bible and trying to sound hopeful.

She shook her head.

"I've been drawing the *sortes*. Three trials at a time. I've received signs of death and of things deadly. A verse on *potencies*—the good, but mostly evil ones. Nothing on *the Unspeakable*."

"What are they? The *scunners*, you mean?"

A smile flickered across her lips. Then, in a voice that a girl or a young woman might have used to speak of flowers or a sunset, she said,

"Worse."

That evening they ate boiled potatoes, recently picked pole beans and sliced tomatoes. Their stored up rainwater was rancid to drink. The boy, Micah, ate entirely with his hands, but no one directed him not to; then, finishing his food, he darted off into the woods as if he needed to hide from something or someone. Orlin glanced at Harmony and sucked his lower lip.

The man spoke softly, yet defiantly.

"I've had all's I can take."

With that, shouldering his shotgun, he strode off, apparently on the trail of his son.

While Easter took up plates and the leftover food, Harmony left the hovel so that he could breathe again. Darkness beginning to pulse, he built a fire and cleared a place to put his coverlet for the night. He sat and prodded the flames, and he thought about the real possibility that his venture would be a disappointment to Chosen.

Minutes later, Easter joined him by the fire. The first owls of nightfall hooted back and forth, and a pack of coyotes howled dolefully. What Harmony assumed to be fireflies or lightning bugs twinkled their mysterious yellow along the boundaries of the bayou. There was something measuredly comforting about them until Easter murmured,

"They're not what you think."

He looked again, slightly startled that she had read his thoughts, and not only saw that the yellow had become red, but also that the lights no longer flashed on and off—they remained steady, an eerie throb of color, in pairings, like eyes, close together, as if crossed. As he watched, some of the dots swam up out of the water; others climbed down from the tall trees through a grinning silence; insects had ceased to chorus. Harmony's imagination took flight: behind the dots that must be eyes he pieced out small, black creatures not endemic to the swamp. He imagined things tremendously nimble, their twisted mouths filled with teeth like those of an adult gator.

"They be what you fear?" he said.

"Do you think we wanted this?"

"Dear young woman, I say, what exactly do you fear?"

"Emptiness. Knowing that the dark places of night have to be ... *filled.*"

He noticed a womanly grace in the manner in which Easter smoothed her long skirt as she then rested upon her knees.

"I take it you mean demons."

"My grandfather called them, 'the Unspeakable.' They have two voices," she began, speaking carefully as if she believed her words were being recorded, "one like roses, one like thorns. Every utterance a lie. They come out from the everywhere to see the workings of their lies."

"Do they attack you?"

Harmony glanced from Easter to the red dots amassing and then back to Easter.

"They don't need to. You see, they drive a soul to self-destruction—it's as if suicide is the only way out ... *the only way.*"

Moving closer to the fire to blunt the chill growing inside

him, Harmony studied a flickering blue line of the flames. He spoke as if in a trance.

"I sense here that doors have been opened that ought to have remained shut. No, that's not quite it. Your family opened a port hole into the darkest part of what's all around us."

Easter shut her eyes and gently rocked back and forth.

"They're always shadowless, always carrying something … *bottomless* within them. They never cease *arriving.*" Then she raised her hands and bent her fingers inward. "They lift night in their hateful claws."

Harmony heard something not far from poetry in her last sentence; he felt as if the remaining members of the family and the bayou itself were surrounded by the overwhelming energy of guilt and persecution and unrelenting fear. Glancing over his shoulder, he thought of the wild, feral boy dashing off after supper.

"Should we be worried about your brother?"

Easter opened her eyes. The look she offered to Harmony possessed the fire-lit, shadowy color of sadness.

"Micah is lost," she said. "But he finds himself out there. He *finds* himself."

"How so?"

"He digs down. The earth that covers the dead calms his animal mind, brings him peace."

"I don't understand?"

She pointed in the direction the boy had gone and the father had followed.

"We have a family graveyard back off there. My mother, my grandfather, my older brother, Amos, and my older sister, Leah, are buried side by side. Micah, he … at night something draws him to them, and he digs down … and he crawls in with them. Or he'll finger out their eyes and fix a special grave for them." She hesitated, as if a thought had been drawn to her like a moth to the flame. "Or, it could be that he makes *offerings*. Offerings to those dark gods that aim to make us destroy ourselves."

"God damn," Harmony whispered under his breath. Then louder: "So your father has gone to bring him back?"

She shook her head.

"Micah will return on his own." She paused to smile faintly. "He likes fire. He's made ... he's made a *pact* with the flames. I don't understand it—I just love him with all my heart. If I could still pray, I would pray for him."

"Easter? Miss Chosen wants me to take you away from here."

Again she shook her head.

"And leave my brother?"

"Your father can take care of your brother."

"Can't you see?" she murmured, and this time her voice was that of an older woman explaining how things truly exist to someone younger and untaught in all that matters. "My father won't be coming home."

❙❙ How do you live in the world?"

Easter's question followed upon her success in convincing Harmony not to go looking for her brother and her father. Sitting there by the flames, he felt helpless. He was waiting for an answer from the outside. He had to find a way to save Easter.

"I try to help people who are grieving and suffering. I seek goodness."

She smiled as if taunting him.

"Do you find it?"

"What often happens is that *it* finds *me*."

"You're fortunate that the Unspeakable haven't entered your nights."

He waited until he could muster some energy for his response.

"And you still haven't explained how or why they felt compelled to visit yours, your family's world. Your father alluded to something unforgiveable."

Easter clasped her hands together. In her pose was the figuring forth of one who had thought it all through, one who was already holding on alone. Harmony couldn't enter her space.

"Could be that we denied the Word—the Word of God. *Ephesians* and *Colossians* tell us that demons are free to roam. But they follow Satan. They are fallen angels."

"But, Easter, *John* speaks to believers like yourself and

promises that a child of God cannot be possessed by a demon."

She shrugged.

"We prayed. Sometimes all of us prayed from sunrise to sundown. We thought that Jesus Christ, our Lord, would have power over the Unspeakable, over unseen realities. But we *see* them. These are no ordinary demons."

"What brought them?"

Easter sighed. She set her jaw at a hard, firm angle.

"Leah and Amos, they lay together."

"You mean, *sexually*? Brother and sister?"

"Yes."

"How do you know?"

"I saw them. Together. I ... watched them, and what I saw wasn't ... it was *pure*. Their love. Their longing. Their need. They loved each other as cleanly as moonlight. They did."

"Would you mind sharing with me how the members of your family died?"

For nearly a minute, she did not speak. She seemed to be listening for something only *she* would be able to hear. She seemed, as well, to notice that the Unspeakable were keeping their distance, a fact that freed her to hold forth.

"Our enemies look into your face, look right through your *goodness* and your *holiness*, and you hope they won't find what they are looking for. You try not to take notice of them. You must *never* let them *touch* you."

In a matter of fact recounting she told him how one full-moon night her grandfather took his daughter—Easter's mother—in hand and how they walked into the deepest waters of the bayou and surrendered to the inevitable. How they could not be stopped. It followed then that Amos slit his throat and that when Leah found his body, she took her brother's knife and ended her life in the same manner.

"I'll find a way," said Harmony. "I promise you that I'll find some way to save you from that kind of fate."

But he sensed suddenly that she was aware of how exhausted he was.

"Everything withers," she murmured. "It's what they do. They make you tired of living. You must leave—leave before they take you as one among sinners."

"No. I've promised. I just need some sleep."

The blast of a shotgun woke him in the darkness just before dawn.

Bursting from the hovel, Easter ran with him deep into the boggy, piney woods until Harmony found what they were after. He tried to push Easter back, but she pried her way forward to where Orlin Ratcher lay, most of his head having been blown away. Methodically, Harmony went about wrapping the grotesque, shattered and bloodied head in strands of Spanish moss. Behind him, Easter chittered in the bird language she had used in conversing with her brother. When she had finished, Harmony slung the body over his shoulder, and they returned.

To a roaring mutation of his camp fire.

And the sight of Micah cocooned within it, his eyes closed; he looked as if he were bracing against a strong wind. Easter screamed so intensely that Harmony's knees buckled. He dropped the body of Orlin Ratcher on the ground and ran to the scene of self-immolation.

He had never seen anything like it.

Though he went about trying to crush out the flames, he knew it would do no good. Out of the corner of his eye he saw Easter dash into the hovel and return, holding something to her breasts. Then he backed away as she shrieked in agony and tossed the family Bible onto the fire, cursing.

But what precisely she cursed, Harmony did not know.

The aftermath of Micah down was nothing more than a small, charred stump of flesh. The stench was eye-watering. Harmony had to pull away to vomit along the floating lilies of the bayou.

Then he went to Easter and he held her as she sobbed.

Moments passed before she began to reciprocate the pressure of his embrace.

With first light nearing, the swamp mirrored everything peaceful.

The Unspeakable had departed for a spell to the unknowable.

By noon, Harmony had buried both bodies.

Easter had guided him to the family plot, and when Harmony had completed his task as sexton, he stood aside as she knelt by the fresh graves. He could not truly imagine what she was thinking or how she might gain closure.

She had burned the Word of God.

Now the voices of the unendurable would begin their incessant whispering.

After a proper giving of time, he pulled her away from the scene. They went back to the hovel.

"This is what they demanded, isn't it?" he said. "The Unspeakable got what they wanted."

Brushing at tears that had already dried, Easter spoke tonelessly.

"They always want *more*."

"What's *more* than death, especially suicide—the form of death that damns?"

"There's always *more*," she whispered.

"You'll be next. If we don't leave before twilight, you'll be next, won't you?"

"What other way is there? I've been ... *abandoned*. Not deemed *worthy* to live."

"I can't accept that," said Harmony. "I've thought of a possible answer. But you'd have to follow my directions to the letter."

That afternoon, in the partial darkness of the hovel, he prepared her, he taught her how to enter the astral plane. He offered that once they had gone a quarter of a mile or so from the home site they could transition. He firmly believed that the Unspeakable would not, possibly could not, follow them.

All went well, went as planned, as they reached the mouth of an exit run from the bayou.

"Breathe the way I told you," he said, glancing at her, then staring at the glimmering of hopelessness and resolve in her eyes. "Easter?"

In a ghostly voice she muttered, "This, too, is of demons."

"No, don't do this!" he exclaimed.

But with animal quickness she was out of the boat, splashing to the shore, trundling into the underbrush. For a few minutes

Harmony pursued her. Then he saw them. *Felt* them.

The fiery dots of eyes.

It came to him all at once; burningly, it spread through his thoughts: Easter must stay so that the Unspeakable would not chance to follow. Too late he was, too late to change her mind. And too far from the truth that her faith had failed her.

Was this a sacrifice on her part?

Or was it the only way?

In his boat, he stood, a lighted pine torch in hand, staring back into the sudden fall of an impenetrable darkness.

What would he tell Chosen?

Yes, he knew, of course.

He would speak of everything that was already dead in his heart.

BROTHER HARMONY
AND THE NAMELESS FLAME

Over the swamp the morning shivers soft and wet.

Brother Harmony sat on his top step, his head buzzing and that niggle of a line continuing to repeat itself as an earworm.

Over the swamp the morning shivers soft and wet.

Because that's exactly what he was seeing: Nahollo Swamp— with Wasp Heart Bayou being *his* part of it—pushing back at a chill at first light, the struggle a not so gentle one, the cause, he assumed, being several days of thunderstorms and scattered showers, leaving every growing thing moist and heavily sodden. Where the line had come from Harmony did not know—it seemed to have swum up out of the aftermath of a lingering hangover as his splitting headache had butted against the gray beauty of early morning.

Over the swamp the morning shivers soft and wet.

Five bottles of "Summer Blood" plus platefuls of self-pity and helpings of Fats Domino, Little Richard and a cavalcade of old rock & roll tunes forced him finally to surrender to a fitful sleep. Truth be, he couldn't get Easter out of his mind—her determination not to leave her homestead and the buried menagerie of her cursed family. Would she stand a chance against the Unspeakable, those horrid red dots for eyes, those subtle enticements to self-destruction? He doubted it. He almost hated her for her courage, if that's what her final act definitively entailed.

And then there was Chosen.

Oh, she forgave him magnificently. After his recounting of the episode, to which she listened lovingly, she pulled him to her throat and told him that she understood, that he had done everything he could. But he caught the scent of her disappointment, faint though pungent. He volunteered to return to the scene; she brushed his words aside as those of a foolhardy man. No, it was over.

Over the swamp the morning shivers soft and wet.

It hurt more than anything else possibly could.

Her disappointment.

He had let her down.

If the gods wish us to feel like total shit, they decree that we disappoint someone else—not ourselves—someone we care for deeply.

Chosen told him to return to his shack.

"Don't stop trying to ease grief or to aid the woebegotten," she said.

So he bade her goodbye and found his shack as forlorn as the sound of a distant bell. Sister Chaos, as usual, did not greet him. Sleep, however, surprisingly did, and yet, in the form of a dream, painted a nightmarish tableau of crows swarming about him as he sprawled somewhere in the piney woods of the swamp. As the midnight-black, winged cacklers pecked and plucked at him, he discovered to his horror that from the neck down he was a skeleton—the birds of disenchantment were picking his bones clean; they made music on his ribs, jazzy, surreal and unsettling.

Then bad weather had joined the parade of discomfort.

One day a toad strangler, the next, a bear's cage.

In the jargon of Nahollo, a "toad strangler" was a cloud-emptying, hard rain of apocalyptic intensity, a steady, drawn curtain of moisture that could take one's breath away, a pouring down like horse shoes and hand grenades. One day a toad strangler, the next a "bear's cage," a swamp twister or small tornado that tore at the canopy of tall cypress, mangling many majestic trees and blowing through land and water with the savagery and concussive roar of a mystic beast. Harmony's shack survived, minus some roofing.

I need to leave this place, he told himself. *I need to quit pretending I can help other souls.*

In his depression, the world had simply become *too big.*

He closed his eyes and released himself to his imagination: winds tingled through him bringing a respite of ecstasy; colors bled away into a darkness beyond believing and knowing, and the moon listened over the shoulders of trees. He dozed off. He entered a dream in which Sister Chaos was on top of him, attempting to enter him—merge with him. He jolted awake. His mind was filled with sweet disquiet.

Jesus!

The day began to heat up. To sizzle and dazzle. His imagination gripped him still more firmly: he longed to drink the wine of murderers, and he began to feel that if he were a child again, he could look at night more calmly, with new eyes that could find the utter truth.

The plumage of night rustles blue.

Another earworm?

"What the fuck?" he murmured.

Above the tallest, nearest cypress, birds flocked. He festered with an urge to read their signs—*augury.* He scratched his armpits and his groin area; he grunted. Both actions gave him superficial pleasure.

Then epiphany.

Here's what a man finally learns: that sleep is only a secret fire. Isn't that why one issues smoke when he yawns? One more bit of learning: death, *if* there is such a phenomenon, is a rite of passage, not an end. It follows then that a rite enacted no longer exists. Thus there is no death. More. That longing for connectedness, for incontrovertible evidence that oneness is possible, leads only to an awareness that one's autonomy is a fiction. So.

So what?

Across from his shack a trio of little coonies smelled their way.

Maybelline's? Probably. But where was she?

Under his breath, he whispered, "I don't belong here. I need a new life."

His imagination downloaded one: of moving back to Sweet

River, starting his own construction firm, making money, falling into debt, living in moment-to-moment futurity. No spiritualism. No mediumship. No astral planes. Ghosts. Spirits. Or demons.

What wants to come? he asked himself.

One hour later, or perhaps two, an answer.

Sway de Rille and Lilith.

As always Sway was mysteriously lovely, her face bronzed as if perpetually in firelight, her black hair flowing down past her shoulders like rain from a dark star, her eyes the color of ghostly, gray-blue mist. When she had poled her boat to shore, she laughed, and then she levitated, reaching two feet or more before calling out, "I know your secret, Brother Harmonica."

"You don't know shit," he returned.

Touching down, she etched her voice in flirtatious stone: "You want to know mine? You want to *touch* it?"

"Come on in. We'll talk. Bring your pussy cat."

He sensed that she needed the invitation.

Behind his inner curtain, a candle glowing, Harmony marveled at how Sway could morph into slightly different looks each time he saw her—*a most alluring shifting of shape.*

"Your Sister Chaos should oughta watch her ass," she said, grinning.

"How so?"

"Tell her to stay away from Cat Bells. She's trespassing."

"I have no influence over her."

"Don't fuck with me, Brother Harmonica, I know you do."

"Look, anyone with good sense stays the hell away from those caves." Puzzled, he smiled at her, at her curious, inexplicable beauty. "What's your *real* reason for the visit? You *want* something. What is it?"

She narrowed her eyes. She spit into her right hand, held it out to him, and in a sultry voice she whispered, "Read."

He hesitated. Questioned his motives. Seconds later he took her hand, felt the coolness of the saliva. Closed his eyes. Looked into the most vibrant part of her world.

And, ever so guardedly, he inhaled.

He saw a vaulting, eager flame burning within the surrounding walls of a cave.

He saw many things he could not believe or understand.

A blue-green lake sleeping in darkness.

Monstrous fangs in a wall of shadows.

He heard a familiar, yet forgotten language.

"I've never seen such a flame," he said.

She asked then if she might build a fire with the magazines piled near his feet. He assented. She shredded them, mounded them, lit them without a match. She brought flame with the automatic typing of one forefinger. The fire was unlike any other he had ever seen—the appearance of flames never to be extinguished or extinguished only through magic.

"This some kind of cheap trick?" he said.

"No. A nameless flame."

"More like a fucking nameless nonsense."

"Not so." Her smile was devastating. She reached down and petted Lilith's neck. "And *this* certainly isn't." She pinched at the big cat's muscular shoulder, and the animal unrolled like a mystical, Persian rug—morphing from cat into cat woman. Harmony inched his rocking chair back a foot or so. He heard himself hiss in surprise or fear.

"This is one of my lovers," she said, as the cat woman lolled on the floor seductively. "Do you want to watch us do our lover thing, Brother Harmonica?"

Her question delivered him an image of the woman who had made love with a cello there—right there—where Lilith, the cat woman, invited Sway to take her.

"No, thanks," he said. "And I must ask you to stop calling me by that name. I'm known as *Harmony*—the least you can do is show some respect."

She smiled and purred. She let the cat woman lick her fingers.

"But I'm not sure I *do* respect you. Maybe I should refer to you as 'Brother Harm'—is that better?"

He laughed.

"Whatever. Shit, I don't give a damn. And I couldn't care less what you do with your pussy."

She giggled to signal her appreciation for his rather feeble wit.

"You're sure you're not jealous?"

"Jealous? No, but I know that you're manipulative. You've come because you need something. Again, what is it?"

She looked so deeply into his eyes that he felt uncomfortable.

"Do you have the courage to confess your losses? Do you believe there's salvation in memory?"

Over the flame of the candle, he stared back at her. A hand that was once the paw of Lilith reached up and stroked Sway's thigh.

"Confession isn't difficult for me," he said, forcing his declaration to sound resonant.

"Then I'll be your confessor."

"Why?"

"Because if you do, I'll reward you with something that will astonish you beyond words."

Chuckling, he shook his head.

"Jesus, Miss Sway—you still talking about sex?"

"No, Brother Harm. I'm speaking of something that transcends sex."

He sighed.

"OK, I'll bite. So what's to be the topic of my confession?"

She leaned forward.

"Your dead parents. I want to hear your story about them."

His head began to ache, and in the pit of his stomach an icy snake uncoiled. His breathing grew ragged.

"No. I won't do that."

"But if you will, I'll give your life new meaning."

"You don't have that kind of power."

Her eyes narrowed, wild, feral eyes.

"Oh, I believe I do."

"What's in it for you?"

She straightened, then lowered her lips to the candle flame as if to kiss it.

"I need to experience another's pain—I *need* it to exist."

"When I was ten, the abyss opened up beneath my feet."

That was how he began. He had no compelling reason for giving in to Sway's pathological desire except that being in the arresting space of a most unusual woman, he suddenly believed it might do him good. And thus with Sway and her cat woman companion listening intently, he recounted the kind of nightmare that no writer of horror tales could possibly capture on the page.

"I found the bodies of my mother and my father in their bedroom in a pool of blood that was inconceivably large in circumference and surprisingly deep."

As he spoke, the flaming mound of shredded magazines continued to burn. Sway closed her eyes, her face registering an undeniable, yet inexplicable pleasure.

"Go on," she whispered.

"My father, a successful construction magnate, had fired his revolver into my mother's head. She was a poet. Had taught school. Loved books. Then my father apparently shot himself."

"He leave a note?"

"No. He left *me*. An only child. I grew up with spiritualist relatives and with Mr. Took and Sister Georgia Gresham. I put my parents behind me."

"Do you ever talk to them—in the beyond, I mean?"

"No. I refuse to try."

She shook her head.

"Such a man of losses you are. Parents. Your wife ... your son." She gazed at him with a combination of pity and perhaps admiration. "Thank you for that. Now I must repay you."

"Forget it."

He felt that his psyche had been unplugged from the waning energy of his body.

"Brother Harm, do you believe someone can live for 20,000 years?"

"In memory, yes. In the flesh? No, of course not."

"I want to show you something very strange—*tracks*."

"Doesn't sound promising. Why don't you tap someone else? Not me."

"It has to be you, Brother Harm. *Tracks* and *much more*."

With that, she snapped her fingers, and the cat woman rolled her sexuality back into the body of Lilith, the panther; with her forefinger she jiggled at the burning mound and it extinguished itself.

Harmony applauded softly, mockingly.

"God damn it," he said, "guess I'm enough of a fool to go along with this."

Something welling up inside shouted at him *not* to follow her; something else advised him that he *must.*

He was aware of two entrances to the extensive Nahollo cave system known as "Cat Bells," but where Sway's path took them in the fierce heat of the afternoon led to neither of them.

"Are we lost?" he said.

"No," said Sway, "in fact, we're about to be *found.*"

As the path wound up atop a shoulder of rock, she studied the clay surface, then stopped, crouched and gestured for him to look at something.

"A barefoot child," he said, noting that the print was relatively small, almost dainty.

"No, a young man." She moved higher and turned left, close to a thrust of jagged rock sheltered by stunted pines. "And this." She pointed to another track. "You have seen all the creatures of Nahollo—can you identify what made this?"

Pressing his fingers down near the track, Harmony felt a sharp pain in his breastbone, then a curious pressure on his lungs.

"Jesus Christ! Is this fake?"

It was the print of a cat.

It seemed impossibly large.

When he placed his right hand down into the print, it matched the size of the cat track. The face of Sway suddenly inched very close to his.

"A pretty big kitty, right, Brother Harm?"

He rocked back on his heels.

"You fucking with me?"

She smiled.

"There's so much to see," she said, and once again she seemed to purr. Lilith sidled close to her. The panther nosed the track and growled low in her throat. Sway quelled her fear. Then to Harmony she said, "What do you hear? Listen."

He cocked his head. Yes, there was an unusual sound.

From a swarm of invisible bees.

They smelled of blood.

Sway's pine torch cleaved the endless blackness of the small entrance tunnel that, after twenty yards or so, opened into a chamber of weird formations—stalactites and stalagmites. Harmony sniffed at the exhilarating chill. His body tensed. Yes, he was instantly certain of one thing: *Sister Chaos has been here.* And he wondered what had called her to do so.

After gesturing for Lilith to stay and guard the entrance, Sway pushed forward. Over her shoulder, she spoke softly.

"There's a watch fire up ahead not too far. Stay close."

With their shadows as companions, they walked, crouching slightly where the ceiling of the rounded passage was low.

"Do you have any pictures in your head?" she asked.

"Yes. Of living things. Of … a person, I believe."

"It's the one I want you to meet." She slowed. "The one I hope you can help."

Harmony nodded. Warm water of anxiety gushed through his bowels. Everything about the context unnerved and yet fascinated him; everything also felt as if he lacked the occult powers that the situation demanded.

I don't belong here, he thought to himself.

On the heels of his inner revelation, Sway stopped. She turned and looked at him through the flame of the torch.

"Yes, you do," she murmured. "You do, or I would not have brought you."

"So," he responded, "my mysterious, beautiful friend can now read minds."

She smiled coyly.

"Ah, but Brother Harm, *you* can read the world."

The watch fire burned at the center of a circular, cavernous opening which rose sixty to eighty feet in height. The site itself projected all that the term *mystical* relates to.

"Is this the Nameless Flame?" he asked.

She nodded, snuffed out her torch and stepped near to the dance of fire twice as tall as either of them, a fire that burned on the floor of the cave with no visible sign of a fuel source—no wood or any other material.

"This requires a test of you," she said. And before he could ask her to clarify, she moved forward, then walked confidently *through* the flames and was unharmed. Harmony gasped. Something high in his chest twisted and cut at him like a strand of concertina wire. From the other side of the fire, Sway gently gestured for him to copy her action.

He felt his body balk.

"I'm kind of out of practice," he joked to her.

Her fingers called.

"Don't shut your eyes," she said.

And he didn't.

He held his breath.

Waited for pain. Then pushed away the possibilities of it.

And the flames chose not to burn his flesh.

When he reached Sway, his knees felt like jelly. He removed his top hat and, despite the coolness of the cave, he mopped sweat from his brow. He looked at her and said, "Who's here?"

She directed him to raise his right hand and to move his palm close to his face and pretend that it was a mirror.

"I'm sending you an image," she said. "Tell me when it appears."

In a few heartbeats it was there. His hand trembled, but the image in the pretend mirror held—the dark face of a young man whose eyes were filled with an intimate magic.

"I have it," said Harmony. "I have it full and clear."

He heard her call out in what sounded like gibberish, the rapid chatter perhaps of monkeys, and at the end of her utterance the only word that he could make out.

"Moy."

Moy? A name?

He tasted it in his thoughts and turned as Sway directed his attention to the flat surface of the wall to his right. He blinked twice as, quite suddenly, a young man perhaps not even five feet in height stepped—no, more so, he *flowed*—out of the rock as easily as one might enter through a door.

Harmony heard himself whisper, "Moy."

And his eyes met those of the young man, and he knew that he was in the presence of an entity from the supra-sensible realm, a captive of an inexplicable time warp or such like.

A young man from the impossibility of the living past.

And yet, most definitely, human.

He was wary, if not frightened, this young man, naked except for a loincloth of animal skin—rabbit, or so it appeared. His hair was black and quite short; he had a sparse, sooty beard and the shadow of a moustache. He was thin and delicate, and even as he conversed with Sway in some lost speech, the rapidity of which reminded Harmony of rap lyrics only toneless, the young man never ceased to stare at the intruder.

In the few feet separating them was a gap of thousands of years.

"I've told Moy who you are," said Sway. "That you have powers. That you can help his people to escape."

"People? Escape?"

Self-conscious of his stammering, Harmony nodded at Moy and wanted to say something—even *hello*—but found it impossible to. He was rescued from forcing an attempt when Moy, still obviously anxious and doubtful, leaned forward to within a few feet of him and spoke what seemed to be a single sentence.

All Harmony could do was shrug apologetically and turn to Sway.

"What did he say?"

Sway smiled.

"He asked, 'What song do you come from?'"

"Almost poetic," Harmony murmured, and then as he tried to think of a response, Moy edged towards Sway and spoke tersely, gesturing to the darkness behind him.

Sway indicated that she understood. Then to Harmony she said, "Moy says that he needs to go speak to the bear." Seeing the look of puzzlement on his face, she quickly followed: "He means the image of a bear." She paused. "I know you've seen ancient cave paintings—well, what Moy can do is like that only more … more *spectacular.*"

Locked in bewilderment, Harmony searched her eyes hoping to see there an absolute assurance that he was not hallucinating the scene or that he had not gone completely mad.

"Is he—is Moy—okay with me being here?"

"Yes. But only if you commit yourself to helping him and his people. They call themselves *The People of the Nameless Flame.* They are desperate. They are trapped. And they are in tremendous danger."

From the early, early mornin' till the early, early night….

A spinning Earth released darkness slowly, methodically as Harmony watched Wasp Heart Bayou prepare itself for first light—gestation and birthing about to be completed.

A rock & roll earworm pulsed through him.

From the early, early mornin' till the early, early night….

This line he knew. He had culled it, unconsciously, from "Good Golly, Miss Molly" by Little Richard, a song that throbbed in his memory of nights at Took's juke joint.

Maybe that's the song I come from, reminded again of Moy's enigmatic question.

He smiled to himself, but memory would not release him.

He had returned to his shack to contemplate the "call" that he had received via Sway as go-between with Moy and The People of the Nameless Flame: would he help them to escape their fate? And just what exactly *was* that fate?

Images popped in his thoughts like flash bulbs. Primary among them the delicate, almost effeminate young man—Moy—and his symbiosis with the cave of Cat Bells, to the young man a living thing—and, of course, his relationship with Sway. She had explained that she had known Moy and his people for nearly a year, but had kept her secret until she saw that Moy needed help, the kind of help that a spiritualist, an occultist might be able to provide.

Did Sway love Moy?

Perhaps. She certainly wanted to protect him and his people.

Did Moy love Sway?

Harmony did not know.

In the supra-sensible realm, what, precisely, was possible?

Stunning artwork, for one thing. Harmony let himself return to the moment in the cave in which Sway coaxed Moy into a display of his artistry. Harmony had looked on in awe as the young man had pressed his right hand into the Nameless Flame and had kept it there for several seconds. Then he had turned to a blank wall and had wiggled his fingers near the surface—perhaps, as well, he had muttered something virtually inaudible. And then. And then the blackened figures had emerged, seemingly from *beneath* the surface, like a palimpsest they had flowed and shaped themselves: deer and smaller animals, a giant sloth, bears, wolves—one could have filled an ark with them.

Moy had led him into the next room of the cave, and there the figure of the huge, spirit bear loomed, eight to ten feet in height, a fearsome creature and apparently the one the young man sought out for advice.

"This is all beyond remarkable," Harmony had said to Sway.

"There's more," she said.

They followed Moy still deeper into the cave, and Harmony marveled that, despite the growing lack of air, Sway's pine torch burned brightly.

"His art," said Harmony, "is both magic *and* poetry—*the poetry of deep time.*"

"Yes," said Sway, "that's exactly what it is. But now you must see the great enemy of his people." She had gestured for him to observe Moy's creation of a new figure.

It was black and shimmered and filled most of the wall.

"This the one that made the tracks outside?" said Harmony.

Sway nodded.

"They call it *The One Beast.* It lives in a remote area of the cave, and from time to time it prowls and hunts, seeking not to prey upon Moy's people—not to eat them, I mean—but rather to kill and mutilate them in a manner that horrifies the survivors."

Harmony had stared at the monstrous cat as Sway explained that it was a prehistoric jaguar, yet it was pure black and three times as large as jaguars now living in Central and South

America. As Moy had pulled its image from within the wall, the beast had appeared to breathe.

A swamp fowl cried, and with that sound Harmony returned to the living moment. He got up from the steps leading into his shack and went immediately to speak to Sister Chaos. At her door, he exclaimed, "I know where you've been. Now here's a warning: Stay away from Cat Bells." He hesitated. Additional words welled up: "You don't belong there. It's a dangerous place." He did not wait for her to respond.

Next he filled a backpack with food, water, a high beam flashlight and a few other supplies he might need should he decide to stay at the cave. He struck off to visit Took who made him a cup of strong, slightly bitter, swamp-root coffee, and Harmony told him that he was about to take on an occult task more demanding than any other he had ever contemplated.

"You best gone ta see Sister Georgia—she might could hep ya. You need better see her real soon."

And that's what he did.

Her lightless bedroom was almost as dark as Cat Bells cave. The woman he had known and loved so long and so totally had shriveled, her face had blackened such that it resembled a prune. In her comatose condition, tended to now by several youngish women, she was living out a parable of care. Transition into the whatever is beyond filled the room as a ticking clock.

Leaning over her, Harmony reached under the covers, found her small, monkeyish hand and held it. Though he did not share all of the specifics of his encounter with Sway and Moy and The People of the Nameless Flame, he did petition her for words that might empower him, for advice that might carry him into the heart of a very difficult task.

The old woman seemed nothing more than a distant, distant heartbeat.

He waited.

Her young caretakers came and went.

And just as he was about to release her hand and go on his way, he *felt*—rather than *heard*—a saying that years ago had emerged as the mantra of their spiritualist community.

Roll the stone away.

That was her message.

He squeezed her hand. Then the reality of his gesture sobered him, for it meant two things at once: first, that she had given him what he requested; second, that he had just said goodbye.

Maybe forever.

Roll the stone away.

No, it was not a reference to the stone supposedly that had closed off the burial place of Jesus Christ—this stone was much more abstract: it was the stone of doubt that sometimes would block a spiritualist and psychic from exercising his or her full powers.

One had to summon up a daemonic will to roll it away.

Thinking of that demand, Harmony headed towards his appointment with the unknown. Sway and Lilith met him at the hidden entrance to the cave. The mysterious young woman guided him to where, once again, he was required to walk through the watch fire. When he emerged, Moy was there, no expression on his face, and yet something in his eyes. Was it something welcoming? Harmony could not be certain.

"Does your return mean that you're agreeing to help?" said Sway.

Harmony glanced from her to Moy, who was standing preternaturally still.

"It does," he heard himself say in a voice that he did not own. "I'll shake hands on it."

Extending his right hand, he nodded at the young man who looked at the hand as if it were a foreign object. He turned to Sway, said a few words to which she responded in a serious tone. Then he offered Harmony both of his hands, palms up, and Sway explained that the gesture was one of acceptance and understanding. Harmony matched palm for palm, not touching, and yet in the friendly space between the two men, something was forged—a strange, inexplicable bond.

"Moy wants for you to meet his people," said Sway.

"I'd like that," said Harmony. "I'd be honored."

He removed his top hat and held it at his waist.

Moy stepped forward and cautiously brushed his fingertips across the brim. Harmony studied him—he would have given his soul to know what this shy, ethereal young man from so long, long ago was thinking.

Gently, almost lovingly, Sway put her hand on Harmony's shoulder.

"I have a new name for you—from this point on you'll be known as *Brother Do-No-Harm*. How do you like that?"

Harmony grinned.

"I'm cool with it."

He saw her eyes meet Moy's. To each other, they seemed to offer a "tell"—a secret, beyond-the-purview of language closeness. Seeing it, Harmony suddenly committed himself as completely as possible to performing whatever might be asked of him.

When all six of them had emerged from the opprobrious darkness of the cavity in the wall, Harmony's heart pounded so loudly that he could barely hear Sway's translation of Moy's introduction to them.

The People of the Nameless Flame.

Moy's tribe.

Moy's family.

A fire brand of three words burned in Harmony's thoughts as he gazed at them, words that characterized the assemblage: *helpless, doomed, hopeful.*

He knew somehow that they had been told that he would be their savior.

There were six in all: ragged, dirty, smelly and, above all, frightened down deep into their bones. First, a boy and a girl— Harmony guessed them to be no more than six or seven—dark hair, dark eyes and a feral wariness about them. The boy was known as *Son of the Wall*, the girl, *She of All Flames*; they were brother and sister. Their mother, quite thin and clad in many skins and furs, possessed a name that translated as *Eaten By Grief.* Her face of runnels was the saddest Harmony had ever seen. Then a young man and a woman who were lashed together with some kind of vine, wrist to wrist. The sight of them made Harmony cringe. Sway, through Moy, explained to him that the two young people, not older than fourteen or fifteen, were largely unable to sleep. Though not brother and sister, they shared horrific anxieties. *Born of Anger* was how the young man was called; the young woman was *One Who Sighs and Screams*. They had lost their parents to *the Long Rest* that translated as death, but the true source of their pathology seemed unknowable.

The final member of the tribe fascinated Harmony beyond the others.

She seemed too old to calculate in terms of years. Her face, her long hair, even her eyes appeared to have been painted with a patina of gray dust, and she appeared so fragile that it sounded as if her bones were breaking with each movement she made, each tentative step she took.

Breath of Shadows they called her. It was thought that she heard "voices" from the everywhere of the cave—voices of warning, premonitions, especially ones that connected the tribe to The One Beast. As a result, she was venerated for more than her age.

Harmony immediately felt an occult symbiosis with her.

"And now," said Sway, "Moy wants you to view his parents."

More to himself than to Sway, Harmony whispered, "View?"

After they had moved a few yards farther into the cave, he could see, in the torchlight, that Moy had squatted down near two pits no more than three feet in depth and the size of an adult person in length. One pit was empty, the other filled with desiccated rags or skins. Leaning down closer, Harmony listened to Moy's soft chant and studied the long, thin pile.

Then his eyes widened.

At the far end of the pit, he saw two skulls.

From there he pieced out that the two bodies had virtually fused.

"How?" he said, glancing up over his shoulder at Sway.

"The One Beast."

He wanted to tell Moy that he was sorry; instead, his attention was drawn to the empty pit only a couple of feet from where Moy's parents rested. The young man did not seem to know why the second pit had been dug.

Something caused Harmony to brush the edge of the pit ever so lightly.

A ghostly gray snapshot filled his thoughts.

Two more bodies.

He did not recognize them.

When he rose to his feet he found that Sway was staring at him, knowingly. He shrugged in response to her unspoken question.

Life at Cat Bells settled in; days and nights of routine streaked with minutes in which Harmony felt, intimately, the unrelenting terror of The People of the Nameless Flame. They forged on bravely. For Harmony, who had taken up residence with them and with Sway and Lilith, there were many questions and, as always, nagging doubts regarding how he might help this tribe of innocents.

While Moy was off hunting outside the cave, Harmony would often quiz Sway about the tribe: How had they become trapped in the twenty-first century? How truly human were they? How had she learned their language? What possible future could they have?

Sway would smile sadly and murmur, "I can't say."

But she did know that they were survivors. They had fashioned a few weapons—spears and crude knives chipped out from the cave rocks. She knew that Moy was a skilled hunter, that he could leave the cave and go out into Nahollo and bring back game—rabbits, squirrels and the occasional deer. The tribe ate fish and berries and any wild fruit available, and Sway admitted that she often brought them food from the modern world, though she feared, at times, that it might sicken them.

Beyond his many questions, Harmony observed the members of the tribe. The two children enchanted him. The boy, Son of the Wall, had an amazing ability to lower himself to all fours and to race as fast as a dog or a coyote; most extraordinary, however, was his capacity to disappear into a wall as if it were a cloud or mist even as he was moving at top speed. It was stunning to watch. His sister, She of All Flames, felt no effects of fire. He had seen her thrust her bare hands or bare feet into roaring flames and hold them there—no burning flesh, no pain, only an indescribable delight, seemingly the only one available to her.

When not tending the cooking-fire or piecing together skins and furs for clothes, Eaten By Grief would steal away into the shadows and sob; seeing her, Harmony would feel an over-whelming urge to comfort her. But, following upon Sway's advice, he held back. At times, Eaten By Grief, who had lost her husband and a sister to The One Beast, was able to quiet Born of Anger and the One Who Sighs and Screams, both of whom spent many hours railing against the darkness and real as well as imaginary fears.

Most of all, Harmony was drawn to Breath of Shadows, for the old woman seemed, indeed, to possess psychic powers including an uncanny ability to inform the tribe what, precisely, Moy would return with from his hunt. Harmony felt that, in terms he could not fully articulate, Breath of Shadows *knew* him; he would catch her gazing at him with a look that signaled that she knew his arrival would either save them or destroy them. During the long nights in the cave, he would awaken and notice that the open eye of the old woman would be glittering eerily.

As tensions thickened, Moy and Sway, as if preparing Harmony for his salvific task, showed him other—and many of them forbidden—areas of the cave. Moy displayed an almost surreal interest in Harmony's high beam flashlight, calling it *Cold Light* and, through Sway, asking Harmony whether the object was alive. They ventured ever deeper into the cave. A litany of spots on an invisible map emerged: *A Hiding Place You Cannot Name, Where Something Comes To Meet Us,* and an area farthest from the Nameless Fire: *The Black at the Far End.*

"Now we'll show you the most sacred site of all," Sway cautioned. "Prepare yourself." Something in her voice provoked a hardening of his resolve. To himself he repeated the old mantra Sister Georgia had gifted him with: *Roll the Stone Away.* It helped, and yet when their trek had taken them one hundred yards or more down into the bowels of the cave system, he was not prepared to see the magnificent lake that he had glimpsed once in a brief, psychic flash. It was a blue-green body of water sleeping in darkness except for, inexplicably, a light shining up from its depths to load the surface with a macabre glow.

The tribe called the lake, *Where Everything Begins Anew.*

A ragged circle, it was some five hundred feet in circumference, very shallow near the shore, but quite possibly bottomless in the center areas. On the mysterious lake, from two boats hollowed out from trees, the ancient people fished for a ghostly form of rainbow trout, a special treat for them.

And on the rocky shore Sway explained to Harmony what the tribe had been looking for—an escape passage, the name of which translated as *The Sudden Revealed Always.* They apparently believed that somewhere along and within the surrounding wall they would, one day, locate a passageway, a secret run, along which they would boat back into their own time.

"This can't be," he said to her.

"No," she responded. "It can't. But they believe it, and so do I. They need your help to find it, and you have to do it before The One Beast eliminates them."

When they had finished discussing the grim situation, Harmony looked into Moy's eyes and saw, more clearly than before, the obvious reality: his prehistoric tribe had few if any options. They could not live in the Nahollo of 2015 among modern humans. *The Sudden Revealed Always* had to exist. It had to. Their only way out.

Harmony had to try with every fiber of his psyche to help them.

Roll the Stone Away.

But could he?

They took one of the boats and sailed the astonishing lake.

They circled it with Harmony studying the walls, concentrating his special powers to locate a supernatural opening.

He found none.

But he assured Moy and Sway that he would keep trying.

That night, back at the tribal campsite, Harmony and the others were awakened by a cacophony of sound, a seemingly never ending echo centered on a primal, feline scream.

The One Beast.

Harmony stirred, and Sway assisted Eaten By Grief in calming and assuaging the fears of the younger tribe members. Looking on, Harmony suddenly found himself meeting the eyes of Breath of Shadows.

In her dark imaginings he realized that he must act immediately.

Harmony rose, and with his high beam in hand, he went to visit the spirit bear—not to talk with him but rather to activate in him a protective essence, a psychic defense against The One Beast.

He believed it would work.

In summary fashion, he related his plan to Sway and, through her, to Moy. Neither appeared to hold out much hope for his exercise of volition, and yet they made no effort to dissuade him.

To his pleasant surprise, the spirit bear responded to his call, growling free of the wall where Moy had first brought him to life. High beam in hand, and with the spirit bear lumbering along at his shoulder, Harmony sought out The Black at the Far End—his supersensory capacity told him to search there as the potential lair of The One Beast. As they approached the opprobrious area, he felt that the spirit bear was holding back somewhat.

With a pat of his hand, he encouraged its monstrous nothingness.

You must make The One Beast leave.

That was the focus of his "thoughtform" to the bear, though he could not be certain that the communication found its way to the animal's primitive consciousness.

At the narrow entrance to The Black at the Far End, Harmony discovered that his beam could not penetrate the unimaginable darkness. Suddenly then, realizing the almost comic absurdity of what he was attempting, he whispered to the spirit bear, "This is not a safe place."

They stood in a ferocious silence.

Vaulting above them was a rocky wall tricked out with ledges.

Pushing beyond all good judgment, Harmony did not turn back.

"Let's do this," he said to the spirit bear, but even as he did a blood-curdling snarl drifted down from above them. Retreating a few feet to see the source of the sound, Harmony saw large, yellow eyes flecked with amber.

The One Beast.

A shimmering blackness within the darkness.

He stared at those eyes, windows into certain death.

His breath caught. His heart triphammered.

He reached for the spirit bear.

And nothing was there.

One day later, still awash in disappointment and defeat, Harmony sat with Sway. Hour by hour he had witnessed how fond of and committed to Moy and his tribe she was.

"I'm sorry," he told her. "I've seen psychic defense work. In this case, The One Beast was more than the spirit bear could bring himself to face. It wasn't cowardice. It was survival or maybe just good sense."

Sway understood.

And he could see that some new, almost mechanical anxiety held her in its grip. In the chill of her fears he could hear a ticking clock.

"Do-No-Harm, know that Moy and The People of the Nameless Flame have made a final choice. They believe it's their only choice—I haven't been able to talk them out of it." She paused to gather herself. "They plan to go down to the lake and, as a tribe, end their lives." She touched his wrist. "They don't blame you, and neither do I."

The threatening screams of The One Beast had grown in volume as, after several hours had passed, Harmony joined Moy's tribe and Sway and Lilith as they made their way to the lake— *Where Everything Begins Anew*—yet now, it was more accurate to view the place as *Where Everything Ends*.

Looking on from the shore with the most profound feeling of sadness he had ever experienced, Harmony was entranced by what he saw: a ghostly ritual of cleansing as each member of the tribe waded into the shallow areas of the lake and bathed themselves and each other; and they sang a haunting song—the song that represented where they had come from—and they bravely held to their task until, near the very end of it, they began to wail pathetically. Each of them. Including Moy.

The One Beast stalked them.

The huge cat of darkness was near.

Fear it was that galvanized Harmony to reach out one last time to The People of the Nameless Flame. He asked that Sway gather them on the shore where, through her, he pleaded, in a gesture of desperation, for them to give him one final chance to find The Sudden Revealed Always—to find the passage of escape for them. A heavy silence followed upon his words. He tried to read Moy's eyes; he sought out the faces of the others, but no one appeared to embrace his petition to them.

Except for Breath of Shadows.

She it was who painfully moved her ancient body so that she could whisper something to Moy only he could hear. There was a brief exchange. Anguish rose from the two like steam. Then, trembling, Moy turned to Harmony and signaled that he would allow him one last attempt to locate the sacred passageway.

The scream of The One Beast clamored ever closer.

A plan emerged.

First, Sway volunteered, along with her Lilith, to distract the big cat so that Harmony could set off in the smaller of the tribe's two boats; Moy and the rest of his people would follow him in the larger boat. They would row near the far walls—if The Sudden Revealed Always could be found, the tribe would enter it and save themselves. Harmony would return to the shore where Sway and Lilith would then take the boat and join The People of the Nameless Flame. Sway would leave the modern world and go with Moy and the tribe she loved, retreating to another dimension.

Moy and Sway held one another momentarily and then the plan unfolded.

Roll the Stone Away.

In the lead boat, Harmony felt the spiritual presence of

Sister Georgia. He felt, as well, a tremendous pressure to make things work. For Moy and Sway. For The People of the Nameless Flame.

As his high beam speared the surface of the lake and the glistening wetness of the walls, he listened to the sweet, silver glide of his oar, and he released himself in readiness for the exercise of his powers.

The boat was like a coffin.

Shadows from nowhere darkened the lake.

He turned once to view the larger boat, Moy as its captain—his tribe was silent, draped in cloaks of an almost cosmic expectation.

It was a long and winding water path, Harmony's high beam a flambeau of night, and always the prehistoric tribe behind him, a sea of hopeful, yet doubtful faces. And back beyond the shore distant screams of The One Beast being drawn away from the lake by Sway and Lilith.

The faces of Moy's tribe.

Waiting. Dreaming of a magical passage.

He heard them murmur what sounded like a dirge. Then their mournful voices rose strong—a prelude to a new future or to self-annihilation?

Harmony shuddered.

Roll the Stone Away.

In his imagination, he heard the perpetual tolling of a bell.

His coffin boat hugged the fall wall.

He concentrated.

There had to be an opening. His powers would find it.

Roll the Stone Away.

He stood and scoured the walls with his high beam. He looked until looking was not enough, and then it was that he heard the voice of Sister Georgia: *See the one stone in the puzzle of the wall—a real stone.*

"My God, yes," he whispered to himself. "That must be it."

Not a supernatural passage or something metaphorical.

But a real stone.

His light brushed over every inch of the wall until his heart jolted.

He saw it.

A nearly hidden, nearly circular stone.

All that was needed was for it to be rolled away.

Harmony said goodbye to them as best he could.

Joy fell upon him as powerfully as a waterfall.

He and Moy had rolled the large stone away, and the boat carrying The People of the Nameless Flame had nosed into a narrow run that would lead them back to the time where they belonged.

There was, again, an intimate magic in Moy's eyes as Harmony pressed his fingers onto the young man's palms. They smiled at one another, and Harmony gestured that he was going to get Sway and Lilith. They would catch up.

All would be well.

At first, he could not find them, despite calling Sway's name again and again. Moving through cave passages that he'd come to know well, he listened, shouted a few times more, and then listened more intently.

The susurration of the invisible bees suddenly poured around him.

"Sway! Sway! My God, where are you?"

Panic rose and flushed his face.

He ran back to the central camp.

He smelled blood.

And then a sight of horror brought him to his knees.

Two mutilated bodies.

Sway and that of Lilith in the form of a cat woman.

Their bloodied, torn forms clutched at each other in an embrace of death.

The One Beast must have ambushed them.

The shock and the chill drove into his body like a stake as he carried the bodies to the vacant pit next to the one occupied by Moy's parents. There was something in the mechanical task of laying them in the grave that allowed Harmony to survive the moments.

Over the bodies of Sway and Lilith, as well as over the

bodies of Moy's parents, he placed pine boughs and kindling that had been stacked to one side as fuel for a cooking fire.

Such a fire would no longer be needed.

Harmony removed his top hat and struggled with words touching upon a transition into the beyond, but language failed him. He lowered his head and fought a rising of tears.

Moy and The People of the Nameless Flame would not wait. They could not.

And so Harmony gathered up his things and left the cave, looking once over his shoulder as the Nameless Flame, knowing that its days had ended, extinguished itself.

He moved furtively through the final space of consummate darkness, found the opening and entered the bright blessed light of day.

Alone.

BROTHER HARMONY
AND THE BLOOD OF ORPHEUS

Sister Georgia Gresham was a brightness passing.

As Brother Harmony stood over a flower-strewn mound of dirt in the Gresham cemetery not far from Took's abode, his spirit bathed in that brightness, one no more to grace planet Earth, but, should spiritualists be right, she would most definitely trail clouds of wisdom and grace in a summerish, eternal land beyond what can be known.

The dear woman had passed while Harmony was experiencing the world of the Cat Bells cave system and The People of the Nameless Flame as well as the narrative inevitability of Sway and Moy and a panther/woman known as Lilith. Language failed to generate any elegies or long speeches regarding his feelings about or his appreciation for Sister Georgia. All that he could muster, top hat in hand and head bowed, was a whispered utterance,

"Thank you for everything."

Roll the Stone Away.

He thanked her for that, too. He thanked her for being among others who had helped to hold his life together in the aftermath of tragedy—the horrific deaths of his father and mother. He thanked her for memories of going fishing with her in local ponds and streams—how she never smiled quite so much as she did when she had a baited hook in the water. She taught him the most important trait that fishing demands.

Patience.

Patience is everything.

And now her bones rested among dozens of other Greshams, both black and white, for the nineteenth-century family had owned slaves, and when freedom came with a shouting proclamation, black folk kept the name. In fact, in east Alabama, it was said that if you attended a Gresham family reunion, there would be more blacks in attendance than whites. But everyone got along.

Returning to his shack at twilight, Harmony crashed on his cot, and somewhere during the night he felt the eerie presence of Sister Chaos pressing upon his chest. Her way of welcoming him home? Moments later, she ghosted away to haunt the night. To hunt. To feed. To worship the darkness. For Harmony, she represented wildness, a thing he needed and, at times, longed for.

When he rose the next morning, he boated over to see Chosen. Her daughters, Violet and Viola, greeted him with hugs and giggles and an almost supernatural acceptance of their deformity. He marveled at them. One and yet two. Were they ever sad? Did they have regrets? Being around them made him feel ashamed of his self-pity.

Chosen's womanly warmth reminded him more forcefully of his fleshly self.

"You look as skinny as a broom," she said, pulling back from their embrace and a longish kiss that sent Violet and Viola spinning off in delighted laughter. "Have you stopped eating?"

He shook his head.

"I've been saving up for your incomparable vittles," he said.

"Incomparable? This is redneck, east Alabama, sir. Watch your tongue or somebody'll throw a dictionary at you."

He grinned.

When an opportunity arose, they stole away for intimate talk.

Without so much as a preface, he told her about Sway and how she had taken him to meet Moy and his tribe. He told her everything. As he did so, he fumbled his hands together and shook his head a good deal and stuttered with his words.

"Do you believe any of this?" he said.

Pulling close to his face, she said, "You couldn't make up

that kind of tale. Mostly, though, you keep doin' the same thing—blamin' yourself for not helping enough. You did all you could. Sway did what she needed to do."

"I really wanted to see her and Moy stay together."

"You maybe a little bit in love with her?"

"No," he said quickly. "I mean ... I just don't know what I felt about her. Same as with Sister Chaos."

She smiled and snuggled against his throat.

"Spend the night, and I'll make you forget those complicated females."

"Best offer I've had in a long time," he said.

And their embrace was a merging that felt as if it would last beyond the grave.

"I have the answer for you, Mr. Trapman."

Over a huge breakfast that included the best coffee he'd ever tasted, Harmony glanced at Chosen and tried to concentrate through a fog of memories and sensations of a powerfully fulfilling night of making love.

"What again was the question?"

She brushed away his remark with the back of her hand.

"Fishing." She topped his coffee, sat down and rested her chin on her fingers. "The perfect thing to allow you to recharge your batteries and jumpstart your purely low view of yourself."

"My sweet love, I believe you took care of that under the covers in the dark."

"I'm serious. Head off on the Talepula Trail and stop at Herm's Bait Shop and get what you need to spend the day fishing. Relax. Breathe the solitude. And don't worry whether you catch a slimy fish or not."

He gazed into her eyes.

Wondered, as always, why he had not demanded that she marry him.

By degrees, her suggestion sank into him. It felt warm and good and right.

He sighed. Nodded.

"Good stars, woman, that's a terrific idea. What would I do without you?"

She laughed softly and kissed a corner of his mouth.

"Only the gods of the swamp have an answer for that."

Early afternoon found him on the Talepula Trail, destination Herm's Bait Shop. It was over ninety degrees; the humidity clutched at his throat as if intent upon strangling him. He sweated and trudged along a good quarter of a mile before a beading of hoots and hollers roared up behind him on an approaching string of sound.

Dirt bikers.

"God damn it!" he hissed.

As he hurriedly stepped off the narrow trail, he felt the thrum of the speeding bikes and could see the wild eyes and shoulder-length hair of boys pedaling furiously, almost daring him to try to block their thundering passage. They were savage and heedless and one thing more: astonishingly free.

A tsunami of dust swept across him as they passed.

"You boys need helmets, damn it all! You're gone break your fool necks!"

But his shouts were feckless and pathetic.

A foursome, the boys were not familiar to him. As he swung at the waves of dust with his hat, he shook with anger, but only for a few seconds. Once they were nearly out of sight, he found himself in envy of them.

They sped off into oblivion.

Without him.

"Kitten's nervous because of them fuckin' ki-oattees. A pack of 'em came through during the night. I could done hear her out here quackin' and quackin' like she does, and so's I put her in bed with me. It's the only time she feels good 'n fine, you know."

Herm's Bait Shop rested its derelict self under two huge white oaks thus making it a shady, somewhat cool spot where a body could locate a cold soda and chips if he should have a sinking spell where the Talepula Trail angled away from Deep Kill Creek.

"Coyotes, huh? Yes, they'd make short work of a fine duck like Kitten. They'd splash blood all over her smooth, milky feathers in the killin'."

Having delivered his response, Harmony took a long swallow from an icy bottle of Jamaican Red Stripe beer, the favorite brew of Herm, who was clutching the anxious duck to his bosom.

"Hey, doncha be talkin' none 'bout blood 'n killin' where Kitten can hear. 'Specially if it's her own blood 'n her own killin'."

Just south of sixty, Herm rubbed his nose against the duck's head, then kissed her smack on the bill and set her down on the concrete floor. She waddled off chortling and ruffling her tail feathers. The dwarf, with an almost sexual leer, watched her go. He possessed a dark, wrinkled face and tiny, black eyes, and gray clouds of hair escaping from a pointed, red cap that an elf in some movie might wear. He stroked his beard, a stringy, gray configuration any billy goat would have been proud of.

Harmony glanced around at the dirty, threadbare establishment, the clutter of it so immense that it nearly exuded an aesthetic of its own.

"I 'bout got run over by a pack of coyotes back down the trail," he said.

"That a fact?"

Herm lived with an incredibly strange look in his eyes—a look that suggested he had espied something so terrifying in his introcosm that he would *never* forget it. His voice, which could be sweet when he spoke to his beloved, wifely duck, could pitch higher on occasion, acquiring an effeminate texture. Harmony had known him for years. Had known the man's bachelor ways and his quirks, one of which was his absolute belief in the ancient practice of bloodletting which he would exercise upon his forearm. Seeing it done always made Harmony queasy.

"Four wild boys tried hard to choke me with dust and 'bout barreled me over."

Herm paused at Harmony's words. One eye closed slowly, malevolently.

"They's holy," he muttered.

"Holy? How so?"

"They ride out of the crack of dawn. They ain't ord'nary boys, is what I'm sayin'."

"You've seen them before?"

"Mostly 'bout all summer. Like spirits of the swamp."

"Crazy young fools is what I'd call 'em." Harmony took another swig of his beer and changed the subject. "Herm, I'm up here taking some time off. Thought maybe I'd go fishin'. Any good spots these days?"

Matching his duck's wobble, Herm maneuvered his bowed legs over to where his feathery creature was gobbling up some kind of small, hard pellets.

"You hear the man's question, Kitten? Fishin' spots?" Apparently there was an exchange of sorts, for when Herm waddled back he said, "We's thinkin' Big Snake Pond might could be good for mud fishin'."

"Oh, sure," Harmony followed. "I used to go there with Dog Hobble years ago. With some of the Greshams, too."

Suddenly Herm spat on the floor and spread it with the toe of his boot.

"We don't like them Greshams—do we, Kitten?"

Harmony glanced away as if he hadn't heard.

"I'm gone need some bait—beef melt and nightcrawlers—and if I could borrow a rod and reel I'd be obliged."

"I'll fix you up, sir. But you got to promise me you won't send none of them Greshams 'round here. Me and Kitten don't care one damn bit for 'em."

"What'd they ever do to you?"

Herm sighed from the top of his head to the soles of his boots.

"It's a long story, an' one best told to the dead."

But Harmony didn't stick around to listen to it.

By intuitive flashes, he found Big Snake Pond and trespassed upon its silence and its solitude. About the size of a tennis court, the pond hummed quietly under a surface of duckweed and scattered water lilies.

Good day for bottom feeders.

Gnats and no-see-ums sprang into existence when he baited his hook with a bloody piece of beef melt the size of his thumb and cast his line out where yellow cats might be sucking up sustenance down deep in the murk and the muck. And then he settled back to wait and to open himself to the mesmerizing daze of memory.

It didn't take long for the past to rise like a vampire.

The last time I was here....

Aidan, maybe seven or eight at the time, couldn't sit still that day; dragonflies and leopard frogs and soft-shelled turtles called his name. He had smiled back at them, and then, as if by magic, he had turned to smile at his father, and Harmony had felt such love and joy that pieces of his heart had dissolved.

That's the way it had gone that day.

The Kid had breathed in wildness. He had arrived where he belonged.

"Oh, God," Harmony suddenly choked. "My son ... oh, God ... where did you go? What happened to you? Why can't I contact you?"

No sobbing. Just tears rolling freer and more smoothly than sweat.

Harmony sat down hard. Forgot about his line.

More of the past marched into his moments. His parents ghosted to mind.

Pressing his face into his hands, Harmony stammered, "Why did he do it?"

After all these years the question remained as fresh and vital as ever: *Why had his father killed his mother and then himself?*

A half dozen possibilities—perhaps more—had been stuffed down his throat, and yet none had been convincing to him. But there, in the heat and the solitude of Big Snake Pond, another reading emerged.

Secrets.

His successful father had always been enamored of secrets. He relished the fact that most people around Sweet River, Alabama, could never quite figure him out. Murder and suicide? It resonated as one massive secret.

Aidan, too?

Was vanishing *his* secret?

An hour later, having released three fingerling yellow cats, Harmony downed two beers courtesy of Herm, and then, under the influence of a slight buzz, he packed up his gear and decided to hike a bit, visit old haunts.

Two hours later, with daylight watering thinly, he began searching for the main path of the Talepula Trail. An hour later, he did not panic, but he did find himself puzzled, for nothing seemed as familiar as it should have.

Most of another hour passed.

And a necessarily wordless whispering held his attention.

A rapid glancing about at the approach of shadows, and words jumped from his lips: "Jesus Christ, am I lost?"

It was not a question that a man somewhere in the vast Nahollo Swamp ever wanted to confront.

When a twilight breeze kicked up, Harmony received an ear-worm: *many a breeze is like my son....*

Words out of the everywhere.

"How the fuck did I manage to do this?" he muttered sharply to himself.

He pushed on, edging along a stretch of Deep Kill Creek until he saw a manifestation of hope: a campfire blazing with promise some fifty yards away. Through the gathering darkness the distant flames were all he could see, but by no means *all* that one could see.

Who on earth would be out here?

His brain kept giggling anxiously with the prodding of that question.

Then his carefully measured approach brought him close enough to see and hear, and when he pieced together the scattered bits of reality, he knew: it was the four boys. The dirt bikers.

He tensed when he saw that one boy had risen and was looking his way.

Following that, an involuntary shiver took hold of him when that same boy called out, "Come on in—we've been waiting for you."

Harmony almost turned and ran.

Almost.

"You found yourselves a good bike path," he said. Minutes after he'd introduced himself, Harmony settled in with the long-haired boys, their faces bronzed by the firelight. They wore leather leggings and rough textured cotton shirts and low cut boots, gear he did not recognize.

"No. It's a divine trace," said the one known as "Lucian," who claimed to be thirteen.

"And neverending," said another of the boys, this one called "Ponto," the same age as Lucian.

The youngest boy, "Koya," merely giggled as if to stop himself from divulging some secret. The oldest—and obvious leader of the group, the one who had invited him to join them—was known as "Volo," a magnificently handsome lad of fifteen, who listened so deeply to the small-talk exchanges that Harmony was in awe of him.

"Boys, I've got to ask you something. What did you mean earlier when you said you'd been waiting for me?"

Harmony directed his question to Volo, who stared into the fire for a long run of seconds before saying, "We have the ability to see everything *within* life itself, even the mystical. We're always waiting for what wants to come."

"Especially strangers," said Lucian.

"Even death," said Ponto, "or what, for you, passes as death."

Koya giggled. His eyes twinkled.

In turn, Harmony met the eyes of each of them. A quiet fear whispered into his breath.

"Who are you?"

"We're *daemons*," said Lucian.

"We walk on smoke," said Ponto.

And at that moment, Harmony would not have been surprised had one of them literally performed such a feat. But once again he turned towards Volo for the final word.

The wondrous boy's voice strolled softly through Harmony's awareness.

"We're blood—the blood of Orpheus. We drew you to us because you have experienced *loss* ... so very much of it."

Rocking back on his heels as he squatted near the fire, Harmony recalled Orpheus as the god of transformations and transformative powers, the god who understood the hypnotic force of music—the god who epitomized the creative individual who can remake himself.

"But Orpheus isn't *real*," he murmured, and instantly regretted his comment.

It seemed that every molecule in each of the boys momentarily froze. The three younger ones cast their attention to Volo who appeared to have surrendered himself to the night sky. The stars were illuminated and glowed like a carefully carried candle; he was captive to that mysterious consultation with self that occurs when one must communicate most sincerely with another soul. Prelude to a moment of doubt or even panic. His body reached out close to the edge of a fearful abyss.

Volo was inside an outer darkness.

And then he spoke.

"Don't assume," he said, "that *we* need something from *you*. Orpheus sent us because *you* need something from *us*."

His voice reedy because he could barely breathe, Harmony responded.

"And what is that?"

"You need to learn how to do what we do best."

Impatient, unnerved, Harmony bristled.

"What do you mean? Have fun? Raise hell? Kick up dust in a man's face?"

"No. Orpheus taught us to understand why we're here."

"Tell me."

Volo unfolded his arms and bobbed his hands at his sides as he gestured at everything that surrounded them.

"To praise. Look around and praise Nature's creation."

"Praise," said Lucian.

"Always praise," echoed Ponto.

Harmony closed his eyes and sighed. He apologized for his tone, and then he said, "Orpheus—what's he like?"

"You couldn't endure his gaze," Lucian snapped.

"He learned music from the birds," Ponto followed. "He can hear spiders spinning webs and butterflies thrumming the air."

Then Koya broke out of his muteness to join in.

"Sometimes he's darkness," he exclaimed, grinning. "He can make that creek over there stop flowing, and he can make the wind stop blowing. He can do all kinds of magical things."

Seemingly galvanized, Lucian continued the litany of Orpheus.

"He eats songs. Drinks poems. He's the breath of stars and the wine of night."

Harmony smiled, then turned to see whether Volo would contribute. The other boys fell silent when he did.

"Orpheus can become invisible and buzz like bees."

Nodding, Harmony said, "I think I met him in the Cat Bells cave system." He hesitated. Thoughts swarmed. "How many gods are in Nahollo?"

Volo widened his lovely eyes.

"They're numberless. Inexhaustible."

"Are *you* a god?"

"Sometimes a god—sometimes merely a wanton boy."

"I have need of the touch of a god," said Harmony, his voice soft and distant and unfamiliar to him. "Often I wonder about my fate. What's *out there* for someone like me who wants so much to help others?"

The younger boys laughed, but Volo shushed them.

"Your fate," he said, looking directly at Harmony, "comes from within you, not from somewhere out there. You should know that."

Harmony closed his eyes. Suddenly he felt dizzy.

"Am I dreaming? Am I under some kind of spell?"

"It's a question best *lived*—not answered," said Volo.

Lapsing into a fireside meditation, Harmony hugged himself and became a happy thing falling into an unknown dimension of space and time. Only the voice of Volo shook him free of his spiritual reverie.

"Singing is being. In music we transcend ourselves. For so Orpheus teaches us."

And with that said, Volo signaled with the fingers of his right hand and the four boys began to chant, their voices so mild and ethereal, so certain. In their eyes, Harmony saw a light such as one might see in the glittering ore embedded in rock.

I'm where I want to be, he thought to himself as the mystic chant continued, and out of the corner of his eye, he discerned that just beyond the extension of the firelight animals began to gather unafraid—deer and raccoons, rabbits and a fox—and he imagined that a chinaberry tree suddenly, spontaneously grew nearby from the soil of night.

In utter and complete delight, Harmony felt the approach of sleep.

When he woke, he sensed that dawn was more than a promise.

He saw that the boys were gathering their gear and preparing their bikes to carry them wherever daemons, wherever the blood of Orpheus, needed to go.

"Please don't leave," he called to them.

And then the ground began to quake.

The three younger boys smiled and chuckled softly, and Volo pointed to the east. There, as if from out of an ancient fairy tale, a riderless white horse raced towards them and then past them, spinning off a wind of never.

It was a signal.

All except Volo shook hands with him and mounted their bikes.

Harmony ached with disappointment.

But Volo was there with a touch of fingers upon his wrist.

"Go and do what you must do," he said. "Live in your hidden sources. And don't waste your sufferings. Give them back to the earth."

Harmony sank into the boy's departing smile. Speechless, he watched as the four of them hooted and howled and disappeared into first light, heading where he could not follow—into transcendence and the sublime.

In the unsayable, he stood and imagined their vanishing.

He felt a moment of transubstantiation that suggested his identity.

He was Brother Harmony—a now more emboldened soul stepping out from the good darkness beyond the night into a sunlit river of praise.

BROTHER HARMONY
AND THE PATIENT WRAITH

For several days after being lost and found, Brother Harmony felt the mystic glow of renewed psychic strength. Those four boys—the blood of Orpheus—had gifted him with a resurrected sense of self and had galvanized his occult sensibilities.

I'm ready for the next thing.

Yet, it did not come to him immediately, and so he relaxed and filled his ears with old rock & roll and bathed his liver in strong drink, and, towards dawn, he would wake and go the door of Sister Chaos and speak to her of his threshold perspectives. Jazz would slither under her door like a seductive serpent. The darkly plangent sounds of an oboe increasingly served as the after-midnight signature of her musical tastes. But he was careful not to infringe upon the mystery of her, the wildness of her, and when she deigned to respond to his narrative ramblings and his philosophical disquisitions, she spoke in spidery whispers of final formulations and the unknown.

She seemed to be warning him that intimations of mortality might make a visit. Not that Harmony reacted with alarm; after all, he had worked so closely with Death that he had begun to resemble it.

And almost to believe in it.

When Mance Gresham brought Morrison Rainer James, the landscape of Wasp Heart Bayou listened and its late afternoon shadows held their breath. Earlier in the day, rain showers had swept through leaving cooler air and salubrious scents.

Stepping out of his shack, Harmony experienced a surge of something like joy to be receiving visitors. He haled Mance and asked how he was and asked, as well, about Merlin. Unusually quiet and sans a smiling face, Mance, leaning against his stob pole, alluded cryptically to the fact that he and Merlin had been experiencing threats from the darker forces of Nahollo Swamp.

"How bad is it?" said Harmony.

"Enough so's we might could be callin' on you for help one of these days."

Harmony chuckled at Mance's uncharacteristic seriousness and said, "Well, you know where to find me."

And then he greeted Mr. James and invited him inside.

Mance was told to return as soon as darkness fell.

Over sweet tea and cinnamon biscuits, Harmony and James sized up one another and spoke as two souls who had given years of thought to matters occult and supernatural. Harmony liked James on the instant. A man in his late sixties, James was a taller, thinner version of Colonel Sanders, he of Kentucky Fried Chicken fame; he even sported similar attire: white suit and hat and dark walking cane. Explaining that, slightly over a year ago, he had retired as Special Collections Librarian at the Mantis College Library in Sweet River, James claimed of learning through various sources that Harmony would be the only medium in the state of Alabama who could understand what had turned from an issue of scholarly interest into an obsession.

"So you've come to Nahollo Swamp to address a like mind?" said Harmony.

"No, sir. Not primarily," said James, leaning forward on his cane. "I've come for two things: first, to make a most unusual request of you and, second, to plead with you allow me to die here, peacefully, in your presence."

Minutes the color of smoke passed as Harmony, intrigued more so than ever, listened as James confessed to having visions, haunting visions of an indescribably personal nature. James urged Harmony to respond, and so he did.

"When such images are realized—fully imagined as centered upon a living being other than oneself—then it becomes a

psychopompos, a guide with a soul having its own inherent limi-
tation and necessity." Harmony paused. He hated the pedantic
sound of his remarks. "Let me put it this way: there are things
in your psyche, Mr. James, that are no more *yours* than ... than
the animals out there in the swamp. Powers. And often we are
lived by these powers."

James lapsed into thought. As late afternoon began to step
aside for twilight, he seemed increasingly weary.

"But I'm not convinced," he said, "that the entity that has
visited me is *other than myself.*"

"Go on, sir."

"Have you ever heard of C. A. Gladhome?"

"Yes, of course. Gladhome wrote ghost stories. In fact, she
once came to our spiritualist community to talk with some of
my relatives and with Sister Georgia Gresham. I remember her
as a severe woman who dressed in Victorian fashion. 'Corabella
Amelia Gladhome'—wasn't that her name?"

James nodded.

"Did you ever read her work?"

"I recall reading much of a book entitled *Wasp Heart Bayou
and Other Tales of Terror* ... or something to that effect. As you
probably know, the title story derives from this very area of
Nahollo and the Creek legend of supernatural wasps."

"Yes. But there's more. You see, when Gladhome passed
a decade or so ago she had willed her papers to our college
library. While her stories were not, perhaps, of the first water,
her research into the occult and, especially, to matters of life
beyond death is of astonishing interest and quite thorough."

Harmony smiled.

"Pardon me, but our conversation reminds me of those I
used to read in late-nineteenth-century occult fiction, especially
the British mode. Where's all of this leading? What's it have to
do with your unusual request? I'm intrigued, and yet my head,
I must confess, is swirling a bit in confusion."

"Sorry. Even now as I'm sitting here I find it hard to admit
what I've ... *invited* into my life. And, yes, I know, that, too,
smacks of the cliché of ghostly fiction." Closing his eyes, James
appeared on the verge of falling asleep or of lapsing into a

trance. "Do you know, sir, what a *wraith* is, and, more importantly, do you believe in their existence?"

"Well, growing up I was taught that a wraith is the spirit of a living person, one that manifests itself to portend that person's death. As to belief—I'm fully open to the dark of the mind and to inscrutable possibilities. I take it, then, that you believe a wraith—*your* wraith—has entered your life?"

In the tone of a sacred vow, James murmured, "I do." As he sat, he squirmed as if very uncomfortable. "Following up on some of Gladhome's research, I believe I inadvertently petitioned a wraith—*my* wraith—and now it won't leave. I don't know what it wants."

"Have you asked it?"

James snickered.

"Just that simple?"

"Occult matters are rarely simple. But you might discover that this entity, having presented itself as a portend of your death, needs to linger for … oh, perhaps companionship or a kind of community of the inner realm."

James shook his head slowly, dolefully.

"I came here," he said, "to have an uneventful death. In addition to that, I'm asking you to let my wraith stay here or, if you choose, make it disappear."

"Like an exorcism?"

"Yes."

"I must say," Harmony followed, "that you present me with an interesting request. Before I go further, I wish to attempt a psychic reading of you. Would you agree to that?"

"Most certainly."

"Lift your cane. Hang on to it and let me grasp it."

Upon wrapping his fingers about the cane, Harmony felt the room swallow him in a thick, gray fog through which, for several minutes, he negotiated as if swimming against an increasingly steady swirl of amassing eddies.

Then clarity and a slow spinning as if in a timeless gyre.

At the center of the configuration was a ghostly figure. Catching momentary sight of it, Harmony snapped back to reality.

And Mr. M. R. James collapsed to the floor.

When the curtain of darkness had closed upon the bayou, Mance joined Harmony as he hovered over the body of James. The man was still alive. Barely. A pillow propped under his head, he lay on the floor, his breathing almost undetectable.

"What in thunder happened to 'im?" said Mance, his fingers jittering as he hunkered down and stared into Harmony's face.

"This has all been too much for him is my guess."

Harmony shared little of what had transpired. He especially avoided mention of the entity—the wraith—he had seen in his psychic reading of James.

A figure of cosmic dread.

That characterization vaguely captured what ghosted into view.

"Is this feller gone die on you?"

Harmony sighed deeply. He studied the man's face which had settled into a map of serenity.

"Yes. I believe he will."

An hour later M. R. James issued his final breath.

A minute later, Harmony sent Mance to Sweet River to alert the authorities.

Two days later, Harmony sat in his shack as twilight stole upon the scene. The body of Mr. James had been taken away. The county sheriff had ventured out from Sweet River to investigate and, finding nothing suggestive of criminal behavior, had Harmony sign some papers after asking him twice to narrate the events leading to the decease of the deceased. Mance was questioned as well and then sent on his way, pale and more than a bit nonplussed.

Exhausted more than he realized, Harmony fell asleep in his rocking chair and slept soundly until the small hours of the night when a harsh, wheezy voice startled him with a curious chant:

Out of the night came the patient wraith ...

Out of the night came the patient wraith ...

"Who's there?" Harmony exclaimed.

But, even as he asked, he knew.

In the shadows of his shack stood the suggestion of a man; he appeared all and all a despicable, beggarly, homeless creature, dirty, smelly and perhaps diseased.

"You know what I am," said the entity, his wheezing more intense.

"Yes. In occult terms, you are a wraith. And you, in turn, must be aware that Mr. James is no longer with us."

"I am."

They stared at one another.

Harmony's voice eventually filled the deadly space between them.

"Mr. James and I had something of an understanding that I would either give you a home or that I would exorcise you. I must assume that you have thoughts on the matter."

In a cocoon of silence, the wraith seemed almost alive.

He was, indeed, patient.

"I want to make a deal with you," he said as the seconds ticked on in desultory fashion.

"I'm listening," said Harmony.

In the intervening moments, the wraith picked at a ragged sleeve and scratched at his filthy neck.

"I can give you your heart's desire," he said. "I know that you live in quiet desperation because of loss—I can fix that. However, you must give me what I crave in return."

Pinpricks of light fountained in Harmony's thoughts. Cautious, uneasy, yet hopeful, he said, "No promises until you share what you believe my 'heart's desire' to be."

The wraith grinned.

"You're a coy one, eh?" He breathed deeply, and in the act of doing so, launched into a spasm of coughing from which it seemed he might not survive. Then he wiped his lips and muttered, "I can bring you in contact with your son."

Harmony found that he suddenly couldn't swallow.

He had no feeling in his arms or hands.

A few words choked free.

"What in return?"

The wraith lowered his head and gritted the stubs of his teeth, and in a raspy eruption of sound he exclaimed, "Freedom!" He trembled. The shack took on a mysterious chill. Then in a softer, clearer tone: "I want to return to the realm from which I came."

He met the eyes of Harmony who was forced to blink as emotion rose in his throat.

"I'll help," he said. "To have contact with my son—with Aidan—I would do anything. You have my word."

"Patience."

That was the single word repeated often in the days that followed, days during which Harmony would prod the wraith, asking when the promised contact with his son would take place.

Patience. Patience. Patience.

On possibly the warmest, most humid and steamy morning of the summer, Harmony had poled to the outer reaches of Wasp Heart Bayou, his thoughts blank, his hopes opaque.

Some twenty yards from the shore, he stopped to listen to the chirping of a bird the song of which he could not recall hearing before. Leaning against his stob pole, he could detect the rapidly accelerating beats of his heart. He squinted into the thick, tree-laden brush of the borderlands. Heard the unique chirping again.

And looked directly into the eyes of his son.

Aidan grinned as boyishly as Harmony's memories always conjured up. He raised his right hand in a wave and, perhaps more so, an indication that his father should not attempt to come much closer.

"Oh, Aidan," Harmony murmured, every string of his emotions being plucked at once, every molecule of sadness and amazement rattling free within. He stared until his eyes burned and his heart caught fire. "Aidan. Aidan. Aidan. My God, my son—it's *you*."

"I'm here," said the shade of the boy.

"Let me come to you."

The boy shook his head.

"You're not supposed to."

"But I have to … I have to … touch you and be near you."

The boy shook his head once more.

"No. You're not supposed to."

Harmony was trembling so fiercely that he found he must sit down in his boat.

"Oh, God, it's so good to see you. Are you okay? I never knew what happened to you—were you hurt? Did someone ... *hurt* you?"

The boy smiled broadly.

"I'm fine," he said. "Better 'an fine." Then he paused and looked all about him. "I'm right where I want to be. I'm in the best place of all."

He hopped gleefully from foot to foot.

And vanished so suddenly that Harmony ritched forward and nearly fell out of his boat.

"Aidan! Oh, son, don't go. Please don't go."

Harmony sat in the boat and rocked back and forth in despair and in joy, and he shivered as if winter's shadow embraced him and would not let go.

He saw his son briefly on three more occasions, always in the same spot and with the same accepted provision that he would approach no closer to him at any point. They talked, and the boy told him of his life, an Eden-like narrative of ramblings in a paradise of the Beyond, trespassing delightedly in the realm of the supra-sensible.

Harmony learned that Aidan had not seen his mother, but apparently he had often had a sighting of Sister Chaos dashing through the wilderness, more the essence of night than of a living thing.

Each meeting punched against Harmony's heart as if it were a punching bag.

Every second was bittersweet.

Until one morning those seconds were evermore not to be.

One morning when the word "Goodbye" truly carried its meaning.

Afterwards, a thuggish gang of crows gathered where Aidan had appeared; they cawed in raucous, threatening tattles and kept all the secrets of the swamp.

The wraith pressed for Harmony to live up to his agreement.

But the spiritualist and father had had his heart broken and spent hours resetting it like a bone. Meeting the wraith with delaying tactics, he sought out Sister Chaos during the wee hours of the night requesting a cure for his grief. She spoke prescriptively, telling him to catch a crow, kill it, boil it in a pot and eat it whole.

This he did.

Although his grief did not cease, it most definitely weakened.

Of Sister Chaos, Harmony had one further question: "How do I deal with the wraith?"

Her response a laconic one: *Embrace him.*

He did not, at first, fully understand.

By degrees, the precise meaning of her words sank into him—and horrified him, for it truly seemed that he must physically *touch* the disgusting entity in order to rid his premises of him.

"I can't do it," Harmony whispered to his dark, female companion.

You must. It is a rehearsal for the rest of your life.
Her pronouncement echoed through the canyons of his inner self.

One night, nearing dawn, he summoned the necessary courage and approached the wraith and thanked him for giving him precious moments with his son.

Sad-eyed, the wraith studied him.

"But will you fulfill your end of the bargain?"

Lifting his arms, Harmony steeled himself to do what he must do.

His hesitation was as cold and clear as moonlight.

Lips quivering, he said, "I will."

The expression on the face of the wraith instantly brightened, and he leaned into the body of Brother Harmony, and the two creatures from realms of the incomprehensible wrapped their arms around each other and held tightly.

No further words.

The end came at dawn.

From the edge of the bayou Harmony watched the patient

wraith walk, like Jesus, across the surface of the murky waters and slip through a misty curtain and disappear.

Harmony fought a rise of tears.

Then warmth shunted up through him. The source of it?

The possibility that an entirely new and unknown self had come into being within.

It had been rehearsing for its moment.

Now it was ready to perform.

BROTHER HARMONY
AND THE ALLIGATOR MAN

One evening owls sang of things that change.

Perched on a stool outside his shack Brother Harmony listened to those songs and thought about the patient wraith and wondered where he was and what would become of him. But mostly he thought about transformations stirring within, ingredients mixing around for a new self. Could it have been that he finally experienced the spirit of Aidan—The Kid—because, at last, with the help of Mr. M. R. James and the patient wraith, he had become *capable* of a brief reuniting with the one he loved and missed so much?

He drank down sour, seedy wine—mostly scuppernong—from a Coca-Cola bottle he had rescued from a polluted backwash and cleaned up; his spirits lifted in the midnight moments of what he had been and on the wings of what he had become: a soul almost at peace with himself.

Almost.

He thought of an unadulterated release from wishing and longing and willing.

The owls called and responded, called and responded.

He knew their language.

He waited. The thought flitted by that he just might see his own wraith.

A *frisson* emerged, flowed and shaped itself before disappearing.

No wraith.

But he didn't mind.

He thought of taking his new self to Sweet River and a fresh reality. Wasn't *away* where he truly wanted to live and his shack was where he was? He glanced up. Wasn't he much too distant from the nearest star?

He thought of Chosen and her two daughters.

"Oh, Jesus," he murmured.

The wine of being is too strong.

He laughed softly, yet it was self-deprecating.

The moonless night seemed not the proper *genius loci* for poetry, but a piece of something came to him—the only line he knew from the poet William Butler Yeats:

When you are old and grey and full of sleep....

"I'm getting old and still too full of hope that I might help someone."

He raised his bottle and toasted insects and the muted bellowing of gators; more so, he toasted Wasp Heart Bayou, grateful that those supernatural stinging things of lore had never swooped down upon him. Wasp Heart Bayou. Here where his mind could find its proper size.

Can you *belong* somewhere you don't really want to be?

Apparently so.

He stayed where he was, a sentry to the ineluctable movement of the universe. Night crept into daylight like a living thing, always strange, always unfamiliar even though he had experienced it on hundreds of occasions.

At dawn, for the first time, he saw the albino gator.

It was large, an eight- to ten-footer. A strong swimmer. A loner. And, if the reaction of the other gators in the bayou were a true measurement, it was not welcome: *gator non grata.*

Yet there was purpose and identity to the beast.

That same day Harmony noticed the albino three more times, and it seemed that each time this rare gator swam a bit closer to Harmony's shack. And one thing more: each appearance appeared to coincide with an ever so brief sighting.

Of the ghost of Aidan.

Yes, across the way, never more than a phantom dash of the boy running free, loving his existence in a realm Harmony could not access.

Gator and boy.

By the next morning, Harmony longed for the arrival of the albino.

A late afternoon shower ushered in a strangling humidity. The white gator slithered through the bayou and towards the shack. Again, the other gators balled in a threatening gang. Harmony watched, and out of the corner of his eye he saw a ghostly sprint on the far side.

"Aidan! Oh, please, Aidan! Stay! Please stay!"

But his son raced off the way all boys do in haunting themselves.

Harmony lowered his head in disappointment.

When he looked again to find the gator, he saw instead, standing on the shore, one of most peculiar human beings he had ever seen.

His name was John Frances Ledwidge.

Somewhere in the desert years beyond fifty, he was easily six feet tall and thin, shirtless and barefoot, clad only in dark boxer shorts. Extremely pale, he stared at Harmony and blinked his red eyes slowly.

His entire body was covered in hard, crusty patches. Like scales.

The man's heart beat an inch or so above his navel.

Unnerved, Harmony tentatively invited him into his shack. "What brings you here?"

Ledwidge looked away thoughtfully.

"Fate," he said, his voice weary, his breathing challenged as if much of the oxygen in the room had been sucked out.

"Talk about yourself, please."

They sat. Ledwidge cupped his large hands over his bare knees.

"I've been on the carny circuit for many years," he said. "I'm known as 'the Alligator Man.'" He paused and seemed to search Harmony's face for approbation. "I've been looked at so long, and I've found that looking is not enough. The heart must see beyond the eyes."

Harmony nodded.

"Wise words. But ... why have you come here? I must say up front, sir, that I have no power to cure your affliction."

Ledwidge smiled gently.

"Nor would I ask you to." He sighed as if he had very few sighs remaining. "On the carny stem I've heard your name. I've come to believe that you can help me with, oh, I suppose you could call them *final things*."

Removing his top hat, Harmony sat patiently for several moments.

"Of recent I've been much involved with final things." Then he reached out and said, "May I clasp your right hand? I need to see what I must see."

Ledwidge complied.

The blue-blackness of a gathering storm mushroomed on the horizon of Harmony's psychic impressions. His breath caught. The thunder and lightning of incredible loneliness and emptiness crashed, flickered and volleyed.

Harmony released the man's hand.

In the tenor of a whisper, he said, "What is it, Mr. Ledwidge, that you want?"

Folding long fingers in front of his chest as if he were about to pray, the man blinked rapidly; there was, in his throat, the sound of cloth tearing. Almost inaudibly, he spoke these words:

"Somebody to love."

"I see. Of course. Yes."

Then Ledwidge shook his head and frowned.

"No. No, that's not it exactly. I want to find somebody who can love *me*. If only for a brief time. *Me*. As I am. Freak or monster or however one may characterize what you see here." His tongue clicked. "Can you ... can you do that? Can you find this ... *somebody?*"

Harmony felt deeply moved.

He began to shake his head as if to indicate his doubts—then he stopped. Once again he took the hand of John Frances Ledwidge, the Alligator Man; he looked into the man's longing and he said,

"Yes. Yes, I can."

With the arrival of darkness, Harmony regretted his statement.

He had watched Ledwidge leave; the man promised to return the next morning.

No ordinary visitor, Ledwidge waded several yards into the bayou, and when he lunged forward he was no longer human. With a silken swish of his tail, the albino gator slipped away into the oblivion of the shape-shifting night.

Other gators shoved themselves close in on his path.

But none braved to block his way.

Disgusted with himself for essentially promising something that he likely couldn't make happen, Harmony went to the door to the room of Sister Chaos and offered her a heartfelt confession.

He tasted the bile of self-loathing.

Sister Chaos listened, then stridently berated him before issuing a simple, yet pointed directive:

"Bring him a *she* from within yourself."

"No," he exclaimed. "I can't do that. I don't know how."

The momentary silence of Sister Chaos roared in his ears. He felt a blessed release when she murmured,

"Yes, you do. Are you forgetting?"

At dawn the phantom woman uncoiled from Harmony's chest.

Tall and slender and wispy, she wafted into the new day with a muted loveliness. Harmony was thrilled at how perfect for the task she seemed. He told her that he wanted her to meet someone, but that she had to stay out of sight until he signaled for her to appear.

Just beyond the door to his shack he waited, expectant yet anxious, for the Alligator Man to swim into the open of a new reality. Passing a knot of gators, creatures both curious and on the edge of violence, he soon arrived. He tail-whipped up to the shore and stepped from it a man with hope in his eyes.

"She's here," said Harmony, gesturing grandly. "She's inside. But first, there's something I can do for you."

Ledwidge smiled cautiously.

"You're in charge," he muttered.

Harmony closed his eyes and grasped Ledwidge hard at

both elbows. As he squeezed, he could feel the man's body surrender, could sense the onset of molting. He continued to hold until virtually every inch of Ledwidge's scaly skin had sloughed off, flaking at his feet in a snowy pile.

A new man was birthed.

When Ledwidge looked down at himself, he trembled on the border between astonishment and joy. Tears stung his eyes.

"Oh, dear God," he said.

Harmony motioned him into the shack.

"There's somebody who has come to meet you," he said.

For the next two days, Harmony saw little of Ledwidge and the *somebody* he had called forth. They disappeared into the swamp like a twenty-first-century Adam and Eve with every tree one of life if not knowledge.

Pleased beyond words, Harmony basked in self-congratulatory sunlight.

And drank in gallons of soul-sustaining amazement through the vessel of fleeting glimpses he received of Aidan. The Kid. And though his son never approached closer than the distance from home plate to second base, it did not matter.

Harmony was besotted.

He laughed. He cried. He watched until watching nearly blinded him.

From dawn to twilight and back again.

Moment-to-moment futurity.

Over and over he thanked Sister Chaos for her suggestion.

For her belief in him—the dead wild talent within him she unearthed.

Hours upon hours Wasp Heart Bayou orbited the great Nahollo Swamp, every minute summer-deep with autumn nowhere in sight.

On the third day of a magnificently dark fairy tale, *The End* waited as narrative inevitability.

It was a muggy afternoon that found Ledwidge and Harmony facing one another in the shack.

"I call her 'Chita'—she likes the name. I don't know why."

"Because you gave it to her," said Harmony.

He saw heartbreak in the eyes of the Alligator Man, the blackness of dilation. He also saw that the crusty, scaly, rough skin patches had returned. Something endemic to the man's condition would not release him.

"I want to thank you," Ledwidge continued, his voice filled with phlegm. He shook his head. "But the thing is—she can't love me. Not forever. I shouldn't have let myself buy in to the impossible."

Harmony thought of Aidan's ghost sprinting through the molecules of heat that filled Wasp Heart Bayou and beyond. *Dear God,* he thought, *I'll lose contact with him.*

"I can make her stay," he insisted. "She's *my* creation. She has to obey."

Sadness poured from the eyes of Ledwidge like a waterfall.

"No," he muttered. "No, this is the end. I have to let go of her."

Harmony reached towards him and whispered, "Please. I can try something more. I can. I will."

Ledwidge smiled a defeated yet appreciative smile. He put a hand on Harmony's shoulder, patted it gently and walked out of the shack. Harmony's protestations trailed at his heels.

His throat burning, Harmony watched as Ledwidge paused at the bayou's shore and turned one last time, gesturing a *thank you* and a *goodbye* all at once. For Harmony, it had all come too suddenly—there had been no opportunity to rehearse a closure.

Into the water Ledwidge slipped as the sun beamed down brightly, hotly.

White scales bristled into being.

The albino gator glided away.

Under his breath, Harmony murmured, "Forgive me my selfishness."

He snuffled once, then quite suddenly and perhaps unexpectedly, he felt good about things. Meeting the Alligator Man had been a decisive encounter replete with the inscrutable possibilities of goodness.

He took off his top hat and brushed at it.

When he glanced up one last time to see the albino gator as

it departed, he could not believe his eyes. Horror jagged through his body. His shout morphed into a scream.

Eight or ten gators had converged upon the albino, each bloody-eyed and savage with deadly intent.

The outcome of the attack was never in doubt.

Blood eddied, swirling torn pieces of the albino.

A sound rose from the ambushers—something rather like an eerie chuckle.

Harmony fell to his knees.

"Why!" he roared. "Why! Why! Why!"

And he stayed there, head bowed as if in supplication to indifferent gods, until twilight fell heavily upon his shoulders.

BROTHER HARMONY
AND THE WOLVES OF DARKNESS

S tars flee the Milky Way. The universe expands.
Brother Harmony, still wrestling with the shock of the violent demise of the Alligator Man, sleeps fitfully and lives in what the night provides.

He is more than he can dream of.

Time and space open, and he seems to remember an eerie howling.

Have wolves returned to Nahollo Swamp?

Or was it the emptiness deep inside Sister Chaos?

"You gotta help us! You gotta help us! Oh, God!"

Frying up a pair of thick, fatty pork chops for his supper, Harmony is rattled.

Mance Gresham, blood on his face, stumbles into his shack and grabs at him as if he wants to swirl him around in a drunken dance.

Both of them end up shouting at the same time until Harmony manages to grasp the younger man's wrists, at which point his exclamations trail off and he feels cold to the bone. Mance, sobbing with terror, tries to jerk free; it's as if he's just made contact with an electric fence. When Harmony shakes him, his eyes roll up, and he collapses to his knees.

The word that fire spears through Harmony's imagination is *trespassing.*

It's the word that fills the consciousness of Mance.

There's more.

The psychic reading translates in vivid terms: Mance and his brother, Merlin, believe that they have been trespassing in the realm of the supernatural—now they must be tried and punished.

The likely sentence?

Death.

Or something worse.

As they race through the swamp several miles to the rough hovel and cluttered grounds used by the Gresham brothers for brewing various forms of hooch, Harmony has an evil taste in his mouth. Within fifty yards of a balling, raging campfire, he can hear a trio of guardian pit bulls whining and straining at their chains, the volume of their barks weak and enervating. Something has deeply frightened them.

Mance stops and presses his hands against Harmony's chest; the blood on his cheeks and forehead glistens. Owl's blood. Harmony knows why it's there: Nahollo Swamp remedies include owl's blood as a protective against all manner of evil.

"You got ta help us, friend. You won't never believe what we's dealin' with," Mance cries as he, once again, shuffles forward.

"What are you talking about? How bad? What's going on?"

"You'll done see. Merlin, he's awful damn terrible off. You'll see."

"The dogs sound like they've been whipped," says Harmony.

Staggering to a halt, Mance shoves his face into his hands, shudders and then mutters, "They sure as hell have. No. Worser 'n whipped. Uh damn sight worser."

Harmony tugs at Mance, then pushes him ahead.

"Keep going. Just keep going."

The pit bulls snuffle and whimper.

Mance pulls Harmony towards a figure seated a few yards from the blazing fire.

"See what they've done to 'im? Look at 'im."

And suddenly Harmony is an ordinary witness to

extraordinary madness—or a brutal resemblance to it. Merlin Gresham sits with his knees rucked up and stares into the nothingness of despair. Speechless, he appears to be catatonic. Physically, he appears to be ... *withering*. That's the word that comets into Harmony's thoughts.

"Jesus God," he mutters. "How long's he been like this?"

On the edge of tears, Mance shrugs. He glances around as if he expects to be attacked at any moment by invisible entities. Harmony looms in his face and says, "Fear only makes it worse. Get a damn hold on yourself." He hesitates, then shouts, "Now, God damn it!"

Mance swallows hard and steps closer to the fire.

Harmony then gives his full attention to Merlin. He hunkers down in front of him. What is evident just below the skin of the firelight is the face of a terrified child.

"Merlin? Can you hear me? This is Brother Harmony. I've come to try to help."

At first, there is utterly no response. Then almost imperceptibly there is a subtle twitching under the eyes. Unnerved, Harmony whistles involuntarily as all that held Merlin's face recognizable as that of a man is erased. Startled, Harmony rocks back on his heels.

He wheels and to Mance he says, "You need to tell every last thing that's happened, you understand? I need to have details of how you boys were attacked. Tell it all. Come sit over here and don't leave out anything. Do you understand me, Mance?"

No life in his eyes, Mance nods.

And then begins.

Harmony mentally catalogs every word.

What he learns is that an unknown force or forces struck during the heat of the day. One pit bull was killed. Both Merlin and Mance experienced a sensation of pressure or a heavy weight upon their chests; they were buffeted by waves of nervous exhaustion. The astral skirmish left them feeling that they had lost muscle strength; they were marked with bruises on their bodies—blue and purple with hideous yellow streaks on their stomachs and backs.

The attack generated the odor of dead fish. Broad

brushstrokes of slime covered the camp area; the fatally wounded pit bull was practically bathed in it. After the foray, Mance had found a few odd footprints—three-toed with razor-like nails. In addition, there had been poltergeist activity: their still had been tossed twenty feet in the air; their guns had been smashed; the siding on their hovel had been pulled free.

"Do you recall," says Harmony, "anything that happened just before the attack?"

At first Mance recalls nothing. Then his eyes flash recognition.

"A bell. Christ, yes. I heard ... I heard a fuckin' bell. Almost like a church bell."

"It was an astral bell," says Harmony. He leans near Mance's face. "You've been visited by *the living dark.*"

Mance shivers.

"What the fuck is that?"

"Something almost impossible to explain. Mysterious elementals or nature spirits. Creatures. Non-humans, that's for certain." He pauses to search for what else might be said. He doubts that Mance will comprehend, yet he continues. "There are beings that live in the invisible world around us—sort of like fish live in the sea. There are other forms of life besides ours that have evolved and exist on this planet."

"Why they after us?"

He pats Mance's wrist and offers only a guess.

"Maybe because they thought you were trespassing."

"God damn it, we sure didn't mean to. But it might could be the thing. We didn't mean to do it."

"I know."

"What now? They comin' back? Can you protect us?"

"I'll try."

"Oh, there's somethin' I gotta show you. It's what they done to one of our dogs. You gotta see this—it's ... Jesus, you won't never believe it."

Wrapped in a gunny shack, the pit bull has had all of its internal organs removed. Its tongue and eyes are missing. Its anus has been reamed out. Sexual parts cut away. But no blood. The remains are covered in slime—Harmony has never seen anything like it.

"Lord baby Jesus."

He whispers those words to himself as if in disbelief.

Breathing harshly, he reaches into the mutilated body and probes his fingertips where the dog's heart might once have been.

No psychic resonance initially.

Harmony closes his eyes. Concentrates.

Incomprehensible imaginings.

Entities made of fierce longings indifferent to human kind.

Yes, *the living dark,* a definite possibility.

He quickly removes his hand and glances at Mance, who is trembling like a leaf.

"This might could be beyond my powers," says Harmony. "All I can do is see if I can generate a protective counterforce. That's about it."

Choking on his words, Mance is fighting back tears.

"But ... we can leave, can't we? We can just haul off and get as far away as possible, can't we? Say we can. Say it."

Harmony shakes his head.

"I doubt it," he says. "Not now. I don't think they've finished making you pay."

Standing over the almost alive figure of Merlin, Harmony and Mance study the man as if he's a mysterious, unreadable piece of sculpture.

"He's in a dark place," says Harmony. "I don't think he has any volition."

His face a mask of puzzlement, Mance says nothing. He can't stop trembling.

When Harmony reaches out to touch Merlin's shoulder, they hear it, distant at first, then an echoing closer. Merlin snaps awake. It's the astral bell, and it's tolling for him.

He is up and gone more quickly than what seems humanly possible.

Mance screams, "Merlin! No, brother, no!"

He and Harmony give chase into the darkness. For twenty

minutes or more they stay within shouting distance of Merlin and the bell.

Then silence deeper than the end of the world.

Then a cry of pain that splits open the night.

Within a hundred yards, they stumble upon pieces of Merlin's body.

Mance's cigarette lighter reveals a scene that sickens both of them: Merlin's scalp has been ripped off; his skull is slavered in blood. One arm has been torn completely away; his chest cavity has been clawed open.

His heart is missing.

Mance topples gently against Harmony who holds him up so that he won't fall. But neither man can speak. It matters not, for language would fail—of that there could be no doubt.

Having retrieved what can be retrieved, they return to the camp. The three pit bulls mew like newborn kittens. The fire has burned down. Clusters of stars have hidden themselves. Everywhere is the smell of death and fear.

In the hovel, Harmony finds a blanket and drapes it over Mance's shoulder and encourages him to lie down.

"Listen to me, Mance. I'm gone to try something. It might could be our only chance. Don't interrupt me while I concentrate—do you understand?"

Mance opens his mouth to respond, but all that emerges is a ticking of saliva as his tongue judders. He dry retches for several seconds, then he eases to the ground and moans.

Harmony moves away from him and begins.

The night walks on.

Silence claims the scene.

For most of an hour Harmony forces himself to focus.

A litany fills his mind.

Roll the Stone Away.

Roll the Stone Away.

Roll the Stone Away.

Roll the Stone Away.

Sweat finds rivulets from his forehead down over his face. A headache pounds within his skull like a jackhammer.

But nothing emerges.

He is not able to give birth to a single, protective entity.

"Oh, dear God," he whispers to himself.

On his hands and knees, he crawls over to the body of Mance.

"Come up, son," he says to him. "This is all on you now. Come up and let me talk you through what has to get done."

Harmony watches as Mance chokes down a soggy biscuit.

"To do this right, you've got to avoid an empty stomach."

He gives him a cup of water and reads a blank timidity in his face. He fights to keep the younger man from detecting how many doubts he has. From the hovel, he brings out a kerosene lantern and fires it up.

"Next thing, Mance, is that you've got to be cleansed. You've got to do it this way. Do you understand?"

He blinks as if perhaps he does, and yet Harmony can see that he is devastated over the loss of his brother and the continuing threat of the horrors of the night. They go to the nearest run because Harmony knows that flowing water is best for ritual cleansing. He helps Mance sink beneath the surface. He forces him to stay under for a few seconds. He comes up sputtering and shivering. Harmony helps him out of the nameless run and says,

"Now we got to create a breathing space."

Back near the fire, Harmony takes a stick and draws a circle with a diameter of twenty feet or so. Then he places Mance in the center of it and makes him lie on his side.

"I'm facing you east because of the Earth's magnetic current. What you're going to do is generate a *thought-force*. I'll guide you through it, OK?"

When Mance's eyelids begin to droop, Harmony punches at his shoulder.

"God damn it, don't fall asleep on me. This has got to fucking work."

He shakes him hard and presses close to his face.

"You're gone to release a *watcher*, an animal form that will serve to protect you. Just listen and do exactly as I tell you."

Again, Mance appears to be drifting off to sleep, perhaps because of shock. Harmony's slap across his face rings out like a small-caliber rifle being fired.

"Lie down flat on your back," he says. "Now, you got to let your anger rise, but stay as calm as possible. You can do it, Mance. You can do it, son." Then he leans over him and says, "I'm getting out of your space so you can do this. Take your time. Think about what happened to Merlin. Connect with that and let what helps you survive come on out."

From the edge of the circle Harmony waits and watches.

Doubts sink into the pit of his stomach.

Minutes pass.

He lowers his head and smells the approach of despair.

A minute later a single howl pierces the night.

Mance's howl.

They are the wolves of the young man's darkness.

Four of them.

They are huge, twice as large as an ordinary wolf.

Their eyes are predatory yellow.

A thin, white cord connects each of the fearsome creatures to Mance, and he, in turn, pushes to his feet and stares in wonder. He glances at Harmony. He smiles.

"Did I do it?" he murmurs, his tone doubtful.

"You sure as hell did."

In the background, the pit bulls cower.

But Harmony is elated.

"Listen, Mance," he says. "I'm gone go get my friend, Dog Hobble, and he and I'll take care of Merlin's body, and we'll stick around tomorrow and help repair all the damage. You hear me?"

"I do," says Mance.

"Just stay in your circle and your watchers will keep you." He paused. "You gone be all right? You good 'n fine?"

Mance chuckles. His spirits are high.

"Shit, yes. I'm good, man. I'm good."

"All right then. I'll be back as soon as I can."

Harmony is not more than a quarter of a mile away when he stops to listen as if for a sound that has not reached him but would. Though he can traverse the swamp knowingly, the darkness seals him from a total awareness of his surroundings.

When the first of the bloodcurdling screams vaults across the sky, he feels something tear in his chest. He lowers himself to one knee. He grits his teeth. Astonishment races through his blood.

He runs back, hoping against hope.

At the rim of the fire the ghost of Merlin looks on.

The horribly mutilated body of Mance, several feet outside the protective circle, resembles a discarded feed sack. The amount of blood around him is difficult to fathom. When Harmony touches a shredded shoulder, he receives a vision. He glances into the shadows. He reads a truth that makes no sense.

The four wolves stand eyeing their prey.

Stunned, Harmony watches as the wolves file back into the torn remnants of their host and vanish like the mist of dawn. His legs give out, and he sits down hard not far from the ghost of Merlin.

Seconds later the ghost of Mance joins them.

BROTHER HARMONY
AND THE WITCHES OF NAHOLLO

"Conjure man, God damn it, you need to walk off this shit!" Dog Hobble's after-midnight declaration echoed harshly over the bayou. A week had passed since the Gresham brothers succumbed to *the living dark* and to a failed psychic self-protection, and there had been days during which, for Brother Harmony, the oppressive humidity had spawned the virulent demons of summer. Dog had helped him lay the brothers to rest in the Gresham cemetery, and then he'd headed back home. Autumn stirred and bided its time—would it bring relief on so many counts?

Harmony doubted it.

It seemed apparent that, via a psychic connection, a more acute awareness of Harmony's suffering had reached his friend, who had returned to the shack with food and with enough alcohol— all of it strong—to drown every sorrow in the swamp. The two of them had gotten drunk beyond description. Had sobered. Had done it all over again. Birds and nearby small animals got tipsy just breathing the fumes from the onslaught of their imbibing.

And then the two men shivered and sweated into intimate moments of bone-deep exchanges.

"Maybe I will," said Harmony. "A good, long, soul-exhausting walk." He felt buoyed from a need to be forthcoming. He paused to toss a mostly sensate glance at his friend. "Did you know I had a sister that died?"

Dog's sleepy slits of eyes watered a bit as he shook his head. From there, Harmony carried both of them back to a kitchen table morning when he was still a small boy; his mother had spoken in a tone of revelation.

"You had a twin sister, son, but she died at birth. I'm just this instant getting around to telling you because I thought you were finally ready presently to know. I couldn't wait longer seeing that I was afraid you'd start, well ... *missing* her in some strange way, and it would put a kink in your brain."

"Jesus on a white, fucking horse!" Dog exclaimed. "I never knowed that! Holy shit! A sister?"

Harmony nodded.

"I got another secret, too, but I've shared enough."

"You sure as hell prob'ly have," Dog muttered. "Christ. Glad you dumped this on me while's I'm not half sober."

Harmony grinned.

"Friend Dog, you know what? I'm doin' it. I'm gone on a serious, son-of-a-bitchin' walk. Thanks for suggesting it."

Dog smiled.

"Why don't you head over in the di-rection of Old Ways? Good place for a spook chaser like yourself."

Harmony stared out towards the end of the night. His eyes brightened suddenly as if he saw things that could not—or should not—be seen. To himself, yet loud enough for Dog to hear it, too, he whispered,

"Damn it all to goodness—that's exactly where I'm gone. Deep Kill Creek. Old Ways. Parts of Nahollo I haven't seen in years and years."

Dog saluted him.

"Conjure man, this is good. You ain't pissin' into the wind no more. An' hey, maybe whiles you're over there, you could see if them witches be still around. 'Member the stories we used to hear?"

Harmony fell into himself. Sensed the approach of something bottomless.

Then surfaced to the beating heart of the moment.

Witches.

"Yeah," he murmured. "The witches. They're no more. Dead over a century ago, I would imagine. But I never could hear enough stories about them."

And so Brother Harmony walked.

For most of a week he struggled under the weight of a hefty backpack; he sweated and whistled and created new paths through stretches of Nahollo Swamp he only vaguely recalled. He slogged through shallow runs, avoided snakes and gators and memories of things gone wrong earlier in the summer. The successes were never as memorable as the failures—why that should be he did not know.

One morning he crossed Deep Kill Creek and was greeted by the past.

Boyhood phantoms reached out for him.

Wherever he walked, he walked alone.

Or so he thought.

He came upon what he anticipated he might find: brick ruins of scattered houses from circa the War Between the States; they had been strangled and smothered by vines—wisteria, poison ivy, jasmine, Virginia creeper, an eerie snarl of vegetation. And then he happened upon the cemetery. Yes, this had to be the remains of the pagan community known as "Old Ways," born in the 1840s, dead and gone by the 1870s.

Bounded on three sides by tall, yaupon holly trees, the cemetery was otherwise a sad affair replete with headstones buried in sedge grass and briers and unknown weeds thus marking a largely forgotten time and forgotten residents, folks who were never welcomed by the other inhabitants of Nahollo Swamp. Old Ways—a darkness passing. Though he hunkered down and tried to read names mossed over and eroded, he could make out only a few and none that rang a bell.

He stood up and adjusted his top hat. Summer was fading, gathering a final gasp of strength; a breeze had the proper touch of strangeness as he surveyed the grounds—here the world was somehow ancient and cold and slow, and Harmony regretted that so many stories would never be told. Who were these folk? What precisely had they believed? Why had they been considered dangerous? Was it merely because they weren't Christian? Were they, in fact, that different from spiritualists?

Harmony had found his destination, but he did not belong.

He turned on his heels and strode briskly towards Wasp Heart Bayou.

Towards home.

Walked straight through without stopping.

But when he reached the door to his shack late that afternoon, he hesitated as something squirmed and niggled along his spine. He looked around as intensely as he could. He tasted a peculiar *knowing* on the back of his tongue.

He had been followed.

That night—all night—Sister Chaos played jazz recordings from the abyss, but Harmony did not go to her to demand that she cease. Instead, he rose and lit a candle and experienced the delicious embrace of an approaching thunderstorm. He found that he was wide awake not because of the jazz piping or the distant thunder, but rather because he felt a desire to write.

A ream of paper, several ink pens, a small table, a chair (not a comfortable one) fueled his ambition to create something epic: his life story perhaps or a missive to Chosen, the longest love letter ever written. Lightning drew closer. He went to his front door and stared out into the chorus of night insects. The storm marched towards the swamp from the southwest, stars formed a bright canopy above him, and across the bayou a shadowy figure stood as if hoping for an invitation.

"Who's there?" Harmony called out.

No response.

Then he happened to glance up at the stars as one fell like a single drop of white eternity from a glass of time and space. Harmony's mind playfully, blissfully created a mixed metaphor, imagining the meteor wounding the darkness as it sliced through millions of miles of the unknowable, bleeding towards him as if he were the enemy.

It created a hole in the night dome above the swamp.

And fell right through him.

He screamed more in surprise than pain.

Shaken and holding his chest, he staggered back inside and barely made it to his chair. When some of the shock of the incident abated, he heard a dusty, spidery, yet distinct voice:

Who, if I begged from the Beyond, would record my tale of witches and madmen?

Harmony blushed with a rise of terror.

"Who is it? Who's there?"

He blinked at a shadowy outline wavering where his candlelight ended.

The voice fluttered like a moth at a window.

I am Corporal Edgar Darkester. Forgive me, but I followed you because you resemble our President and because you emit the unmistakable, albeit faint, fragrance of the occult. Moreover, a piece of a star has just fallen upon you. Say that I err, and I shall leave you to your peace and to the conflicted pleasures of your powers.

Stunned, Harmony lapsed into shy-hearted thoughts of responding to the needs of the astral plane. Once he had controlled his breathing, he squinted into the borderland of shadows and made out a hatless, rather short, young man (barely five feet in height) clad in *gray*, a long, double-breasted tailcoat worn by Confederate soldiers.

"Corporal Darkester, sir—no, you are not in error." Hesitation ensued, allowing for doubts and perturbations to amass. Harmony battled through them. "May I ask, sir, how I might be of service to you?"

The young corporal nodded and bowed his head.

For an instant or two, Harmony feared that the apparition would wholly flee. Then the head lifted and the lips moved.

Like Job, I can cry out that my harp is turned to mourning, and my organ into the voice of them that weep.

Harmony cleared his throat.

"I'm afraid, sir, that I don't follow you."

With a deflecting movement of a hand, the corporal continued.

Because I'm unable to write it myself, I'm here to petition you to write it for me: my chronicle of secret loss—my confession of the best of intentions gone horribly wrong.

"I must admit, sir, that I am not skilled as a writer."

Nor need you be. With those words, the ghost of a man stepped into the semicircle of light, bore in upon Harmony's face and spoke in a weary, though eagerly meaningful tone: *Welcome your invisible self as you give absence a local habitation and a name. Open to enduring words. Be my scribe. Record with assiduous care.* His chest heaved noticeably before ending thusly: *Most of all this: Beware the flames! Beware the flames!*

Harmony swallowed a dozen or more questions.

He said *yes* with his eyes.

And Corporal Edgar Darkester vanished.

But not before leaving a corked bottle, black in color, upon the writing desk.

Harmony stared at the object left behind, yet dared not touch it.

As dawn approached, Harmony shook himself out of a thick daze. It felt as if he had awakened from being hypnotized. His candle had burned down completely; the wax had melted, guttered and hardened. The curious black bottle remained where it had been placed. He found, as well, that he had an ink pen in each hand.

Then an even stronger shock at the center of the enigmatic scene.

A stack of several dozen sheets of paper—in *his* handwriting—pulled his eyes into mystery. His fingers trembled as he lifted the writing and began to read:

The Fable in the Deep

I, Edgar Thomas Darkester, age twenty, looking back on the sad and solemn year of Eighteen Hundred and Sixty-Four, feel resolutely compelled to dictate a confession and a tragic chronicle regarding the destruction of my family. May the gods have mercy upon me for unknowingly setting loose the powers of an implacable, relentless, malignity. Where I sought love, horrors sought me. I have generated, experienced and witnessed transgressions.

I have called the darkness down upon those I loved most!

I fear that I am beyond forgiveness!

Harmony stopped reading.

He softly gasped.

Leafing through the sheets, he realized that he had written with such a flurry that, in moments, he must have penned with both hands at the same time. That thought caused him to shiver and shake.

"My God, oh, my God," he murmured.

Automatic writing.

He had, indeed, become Corporal Darkester's "scribe."

And something more: a personal, ghostly bond had been forged.

Quite suddenly, as the sky in the east pinked and glimmered, he realized he had pledged to himself that he must record the tale of this mysterious stranger.

To a manuscript from the haunted past.

The Fable in the Deep.

After drinking down most of a strong pot of swamp root coffee, Harmony steeled himself to read more of what had been dictated to him. He raised each page to his face as tenderly as he would have a newborn child.

In thirsty sips, he drank in each of Corporal Darkester's words and sentences:

Every life, to a certain extent, is a falsehood and a lie. The fable in the deep is a dark secret about oneself that he or she learns only through living and, mostly, through dying. It is one's personal myth. Perhaps it is one's fate.

Harmony waded into the young man's background, learning that he and three older sisters had been born on the border of Nahollo Swamp and that his parents had, in the 1850s, perished at the hands of a mysterious camp fever, one resembling typhoid. At said point, the four children were fathered and mothered by their paternal uncle, Samuel Wesley Darkester, a brilliant man who educated them firmly in the humanities while not giving short shrift to mathematics and all of the sciences. Primarily, though, he taught them to shun dogma in every form, especially that of organized religion. He preached the gospel of Emersonian goodness with a smattering of Gnosticism and selected wisdom from pagan sources.

Short and portly, with long, flowing black hair and unassailable, black brows, he did not flinch in the face of opposition and harassment from the other denizens of Nahollo:

Give us our daily burnings at the stake: hang us, if you must, in our waking hours until the death within us rises like a new dawn. Cast your cold eye upon us until the full moon in our hearts blinds you. Damn yourself upon that cross that you bear.

The words of Uncle Samuel blazed across the page.

Yes, the Darkesters were condemned as godless and worse. It was whispered that the tiny community of Old Ways—comprised of two other families besides the Darkesters—practiced witchcraft and worshiped Satan.

Especially the Darkester females.

Witches in the blood.

The increasingly familiar voice of Corporal Darkester wafted up from the sheets Harmony had engaged:

Younger brother that I was, I grew in the warm, shadow-strewn magic of my wondrous sisters, and I flourished in the witchery of longing to be always near them. My sisters, goddesses, not witches, revealed themselves each day out of all that is hidden from eyes that refused to see their beauty and their grace. They stood their ground against hearts determined to destroy them. My sisters wore all the garments of the great Nahollo Swamp; they clothed their souls wildly in chinaberries, moss and nameless creeks. They knew the pagan holiness of maidenhair fern and cedar knees and the flaky skin of molting moccasins. Leaf mold and pine sap were their perfumes. Yet, their hearts had to breathe in the unfortunate reality that life beyond the swamp was an open wound.

The War.

My sisters and I practiced being deaf to its roar.

They taught me to live in the country of eternal dawn.

They taught me to see that Deep Kill Creek sparkled like the eyes of dragons.

They touched and tasted and smelled every molecule of the invis-
ible. They knew that Nahollo Swamp was so alive that even freshly dug
graves traveled.

I knew and loved all the varieties of their darkness.

They being ever sacred to me, I walked through the fire of their
lives.

Nearly overcome with the corporal's intimate vision of
his sisters, Harmony pushed away from the table in order to
allow his breathing to slow. By degrees, the renderings from the
beyond were enchanting him—*possessing* him.

To himself he muttered, "I can't resist what's here."

Then he let himself be introduced to each of the sisters, and
as he read, the blood of new dawns coursed through him.

Japonica, hair as red as a fox, was the youngest, she being only two
years my senior. The youngest, yes, but I must say that she was the
most beautiful. To men who gazed upon her, she was the most desir-
able. She loved animals. Once upon a time she brought home a stray
beast, one that was part coyote, part dog and totally wild. In a sardonic
nod to those who persecuted us, she named it "Lucifer," and, much to
her pleasure, she found that it readily became her loyal protector.

Lily was the middle sister, a few years older than Japonica, but not
blessed with her beauty. Pale of skin, she had the gray-brown-colored
hair of a field mouse, and did not tend to her appearance. The great
wilderness was the only mirror she spoke to for a reflection of her-
self. Fearless and a lover of solitude, she conversed with every creature,
even alligators. More so, she kept poisonous "snakelets" as pets, draw-
ing these young reptiles from pine islands and coffee-colored runs into
a small pool behind our humble abode, and there she would feed them
frogs and toads, and she would fondle them lovingly. They were her
closest companions, her apostles, her disciples.

Her lovers.

Harmony paused again. He could easily envision both
Japonica and Lily, the loveliness of the former, the strangeness

of the latter, and while he was instantly charmed by the sketches of their characters, it was Rose, the eldest daughter, who thoroughly engrossed him.

Raven-haired like those women of fantastical yesterdays, Rose was the keeper of all our siblings, watching over us with a secret fire burning in her eyes. Lovely and full of wisdom and charm, she possessed the living lyricism of a poet and the rugged strength of a warrior; she was generous, courageous and yet sensitive. Creatively bold, she was uncompromising and prided her person in self-denial. She was, in sum, an occult angel.

Could such a woman tinged with immortality have walked the earth?

Harmony pondered the possibility, desiring that it might have been so.

Who were the enemies of the family?

One stood out among the many.

Known simply as "Jaggs," he was a man filled with blinding hatred. His face shaped like the blade of an axe, he lived to hew at whatever evils he imagined in the seething riot of his harried, troubled brain. He was a "witch finder" and wore his black cape and pointed hat like the surrogate uniform of his imaginary God. Though he kept a long sword always close at hand, his chief means of executing those who had sinned against his Bible-haunted world was the noose: his hunger to hang souls could not be satiated.

Harmony stacked the sheets and set them on his writing table. He was exhausted. On his threadbare cot, he slept for a few hours before he felt the presence once again of Corporal Darkester—and the scorching flames of a curious compulsion to listen, obey and continue with *The Fable in the Deep*.

Barely conscious, he leaned over blank sheets and wrote mechanically, filling page after page until his hand cramped and his mouth became as dry as cotton. Jerking back to his senses, he realized that another day was losing light. He stared at the mysterious bottle the corporal had left with him, and then he lit a fresh candle and began to read.

Moving in fits and starts, the narrative summarized daily life at Old Ways and featured hints regarding Edgar Darkester's decision to join the fighting, though he held no strong convictions regarding *the Cause*. While his family kept a slave, a giant soul they called "Ham," Edgar was not a true believer in slavery. He was, however, much taken with the indescribable suffering generated through the national conflict. In Nahollo Swamp, he had come upon "mossbacks" and "bummers," those frightened and unfortunate souls who were hiding from battle and wandering through a terrifying realm hoping merely to survive. Such individuals told him and his sisters of the horrible medical conditions of confederate soldiers, especially since the fall of Atlanta and the moving of many wounded from that burning city to Columbus, Georgia, a town of moderate size within forty miles of Nahollo.

Taking Ham with me, I joined the fray and donned a uniform and was promoted, but I was no fighter. I suppose it was through evidence of my compassion that I was assigned to a convalescent house in Columbus, a facility run by a Mrs. Opal Woodling, a saint of a woman who took in a handful of men, the overflow from field and regular army hospitals. I became a "consolatory," and my heart was stolen away and consigned to a dingy cell of sorrow. My duties brought me in close contact with three extreme cases of "cannon fever," soldiers who had developed a violent aversion to combat—they had both horrid physical and mental wounds. Within a few weeks of knowing these men, I understood that they would die if I were not to transport them to a place of healing.

Who were these doomed men?

Corporal Darkester directed Harmony's hand to sketch each:

John Patrick Williams, a wound-dresser in the field, had experienced a grievous injury to his right shoulder; aforementioned hurt resulted in the entire arm needing to be amputated in brutal fashion.

A quiet, handsome, difficult-to-know man, Williams, as the result of a grotesque case of diarrhea, lost an astonishing amount of weight. He was, all in all, a skeleton barely able to leave his cot. He often asked me to speak of Nahollo Swamp, its various flora and fauna. Against regulations, I allowed him to keep a mangy, calico cat. I saw to it that the poor animal received food scraps most days.

Buhler Brohm, of German descent, had served as a guard at the Andersonville Prison south and east of Columbus, but when he fell terribly ill with swamp fever, he was moved to Mrs. Woodling's where I tended to him. In the throes of his affliction, he, also, lost a shocking amount of weight, and yet what tortured him more so were horrific dreams and visions and hallucinations that frequently led to his awakening his companions via the most hideous screams I have ever heard. In his lucid moments, however, he would sing the lovely lyrics of Franz Schubert. I would urge him to do so, and I would softly applaud his efforts. Though an agnostic, I never tired of hearing him sing "Ave Maria."

Joseph Joab Shuggart smoldered with an inner need for violence. Smallish and thin and very hairy, he had the most serious physical wound of the three, for during the fighting at Shiloh a ball penetrated the back of his skull and, I was told, lodged just over his right ear. It could not be removed. He was, moment to moment, capable of explosions of rage. In one unfortunate episode he attacked and bit out a large chunk of the cheek of one of our matrons. Most of the time, naturally, we kept him restrained with rope and leather straps. By day he slept. At night he roamed in an unlit landscape of mental horror. The only consolation is that he committed most of his atrocities in the killing fields of his imagination. For Mr. Shuggart I had two distinct feelings: complete sympathy and consummate fear.

Harmony gathered from Corporal Darkester that the war had "swallowed" these men. But he had refused to give up on them and, in the empty hours of the night he charted a response to their suffering: he would move them to Old Ways, somehow transecting Nahollo Swamp with the goal of delivering them to the home of Uncle Samuel and, especially, to the restorative magic of his three extraordinary sisters. Though knowing full well that she was going against military regulations, Mrs. Woodling generously aided the corporal's plan, providing necessary supplies including a pair of *avalanches*—ironically misnamed for two-wheeled ambulances or extended carts—to serve as transportation. Ham, though ostensibly given his freedom, loyally signed on with the venture.

It bordered upon being a death march.

The journey took over a week, and I must say that nothing in Nahollo Swamp cared about us along the way. In the swamp we confronted a surprisingly different bestiary of life forms—mists, ooze, slime, muck, and rapacious moss and lichen. We feared the usual creatures: snakes, gators, black bears, coyotes and wild boars; but, down to our gritty essence, we feared the unknown. The perilous landscape constantly reminded us that hope does not guarantee one that he will be forgiven for bad decisions; however, I had promised those three men who teetered upon the edge of madness that I would see it through for them. Hold on! Have courage! Will our exercise of humanity to succeed. Yes, the mystery, the secret, inexplicable beauty of the great swamp was beyond one's capacity to comprehend, and yet I exhorted them to listen for the voices of nature beyond the human, for in them I believed they would hear songs of revitalization as well as cries of affliction and sorrow.

I hated it that my words often seemed to ring hollow.

Desperate, I even shared with them the only verse in the Bible that echoed the assurances of pagan and occult ways: "We shall all be changed, in a moment, in the twinkling of an eye." Thus it is written in Corinthians.

Looking back, I inject this: as a pagan sympathizer, I was commonly in league with nature and its animistic forces. However, something different had emerged. Did my three patients alter the fabric of reality? Were they catalysts for dark shifts in things endemic to the swamp? I came to know this: I was no longer a conduit for natural, supportive agents. I was part and parcel of moral disarray.

When the small troop finally reached Old Ways, the corporal's patients were no more than skeletal outlines of human beings—tired, hungry and weakened beyond description, they stared out at the world with horror-filled eyes that implored the air they breathed for the miracle of transformation.

Corporal Darkester put it best: *Despite its vestiges of hope, living has made me suspect that something pernicious fuels the universe.*

With zombie-like obedience, Harmony continued to take dictation from the phantom spirit of the corporal; barely stopping to eat or drink or sleep, he hunched over each new sheet and filled it mechanically as if his hands were being guided by a force that would not be denied until the entire chronicle of *The Fable in the Deep* was recorded.

At intermittent moments, Harmony would pause to read through what he had been directed to ink upon the pages, and he entered a stretch within the narrative in which he became greatly cheered—Corporal Darkester's grand commitment to save his wretched trio of men initially bore fruit. His Uncle Samuel, something of a physician as well as a wizard, treated each of them with an assortment of swamp potions, roots and arcane medicines, including a mysterious "black drink" the base of which derived from the roasted leaves and stems of yaupon holly. But an equally key factor in the salubrious process centered on Japonica, Lily and Rose, who devoted their time and energy selflessly to the arts of recovery.

Living among my sisters again, I fully embraced their rituals of gathering and sorting and brewing—the toil and trouble of all that is vital bubbled up in the cauldron of normality. As the days passed and the world turned, our capacious home was transformed into an asylum for miraculous possibilities; my loving and generous sisters applied passion as a mythic force and tended assiduously to each of the visitant men, and yet, by degrees, I witnessed a pairing off that warmed both my heart and my soul. I observed, to wit, that Japonica developed a special friendship with Brohm. She nursed his body as well as his mind, and, together, they enjoyed the company of Lucifer. Additionally, she encouraged Brohm to sing; as a result, the plangent lyrics of Schubert often filled our twilights—"The Linden Tree" and "Frozen Tears" among many others.

I found, oddly enough, that Lily and Shuggart bonded. It seemed, indeed, that Lily's wildness was, ironically, an antidote for all of Shuggart's simmering darkness. She brought her venomous snakelets to his bedside, and he handled them as lovingly as she. Most pleasing, however, was the fact that Rose discovered in Williams an answer from out of the unexpected to alleviate her veiled need for male companionship. They were together for hours each day talking, even laughing, with Rose reading to him and with both of them petting and giving attention to the calico cat that somehow had survived our trek through Nahollo Swamp. Williams often requested that she read Lord Byron's "The Prisoner of Chillon" to him and, together, they mused admiringly upon the lines: "But silence, and a stirless breath / Which neither was of life nor death."

Intuitively, though, Harmony knew that the astonishing recovery of the men might not last. In fact, he found himself at one point pulling away from the blank sheets and emotionally refusing to go on lest he face a negative twist in the chronicle. And he was frequently haunted by the early words of Corporal Darkester: *Beware the flames! Beware the flames!* What did he mean? Could he have been referring to some perceived punishment to be visited upon his scribe for agreeing to the task? Harmony did not know, and Corporal Darkester would not respond to his most insistent questions. Then there was Sister Chaos who, on more than one occasion, spoke into Harmony's introcosm urging him to end his relationship with the corporal and the manuscript of *The Fable in the Deep.*

But why?

What did she see? What did she know?

To her he murmured, "I must complete this manuscript. I must. This chronicle must be published. The world needs to read what happened here, to know and understand what ran in the veins of Nahollo's history. It's a story that reminds us how things truly exist."

Sister Chaos pulled away from him into a tumultuous silence.

Harmony, needing to bind thing to thing, swam into

candle-lit nights and invited the corporal to direct his hand. What he soon detected was that the boundaries of the normative could easily dissolve, and that while human passion is a mythic force, fierce powers may erupt within a microcosm of danger. Even as General Sherman marched in bloody, destructive fashion through Georgia, the community of Old Ways faced horrors of its own.

Everyone began to have nightmares. Williams dreamed that the sun had a phallus and urinated down upon our settlement and its inhabitants. In response to malignant influences, Uncle Samuel let blood from all of us and, as well, administered a mixture of morphine and swamp herbs. Invisible agents were attacking. The other families of Old Ways left in fear, leaving only ours and the patients we tended.

One dawn, tinted the color of madness, the fabric of our reality unraveled.

We barked and yelped. We fell dumb. We shuddered and spun on our heels like a child's top. Then, seized by a mysterious limpness, several of us could not stand up. Other times we became spasmodically rigid until a moment of breaking free to manifest indecipherable gestures hideous to behold. We cowered under tables and in the barn and the root cellar. Poor, dear Lily climbed a tree and could, only with extreme force, be extricated. She of a sudden developed a wild talent for being able to start a fire just by raising her hand, palm forward.

It was a strange and inexplicable business from which not one of us— not even Uncle Samuel—could fully recover. At times our very presence would send skillets and plates, forks and knives slamming against walls or dancing upon the floor or ceiling. I even witnessed Japonica charming a wild bird into her hands and then plucking off its wings. I saw Shuggart employ his Bowie knife to kill a young mossyback who was passing through—then, extending the horror, I saw him consume the poor man's blood. Such moments drove me to the brink of insanity.

The catalogue of witchy horrors unfolded unceasingly.
Harmony dutifully recorded them.
The corporal's voice quietly shrieked—it would be heard.

The Hours Filled With Blood took up residence in our world.
From a distance, Jaggs gathered evidence for a Day of Judgment.

Harmony received the flood of words, but at one point, flushed with the stream of terror that the corporal sent his way, he fainted. He lay upon the floor until light from a full moon poured over him like a supernatural libation. The pool of milky whiteness chilled him. He shook himself awake and, once again, took up his pen.

What follows is a summary of how it ended.

Our tenor, Brohm, having secretly stolen my uncle's revolver, found that suicide was the only counteraction to his increasingly frightful dreams and hallucinations. Naturally Japonica fell bereft. Her grief apparently sought violent closure, for, with an axe, she chopped off one of Lucifer's front paws; following that senseless act, she poisoned herself. On a rainy morn, we buried her and Brohm in the same pine coffin as seemed appropriate. Days later we learned that the ghosts of both of them were haunting the far reaches of Nahollo Swamp.

Lily clung desperately to Shuggart and his exercise of vampiric tendencies. Indeed, I had come to believe that the crazed fellow might not even be human, but for Lily there was no respite from her mental anguish unless she could merge, intimately, with his spirit. "I am Shuggart!" she screamed one sun-blistered afternoon. Perhaps knowing that a miraculous oneness between them could not be affected, she took his Bowie knife and stabbed it through his heart as he slept. Realizing what she had done, she then lowered herself into her pool of venomous snakelets and baptized herself in poison, a ritual that precluded any possibility of occult salvation.

Death pressing at every side of her, dear Rose determined to nurse Mr. Williams with all possible skill. However, he fell prey to the emergence of a most violent aspect of his personality. He brutally dispatched his calico cat and then dashed into the woods where he built a fulsome mound of sticks and branches; before any of us, including

Rose, could stop him, he created a stunning bonfire and threw himself into its flames, a martyr to madness.

The corporal, Uncle Samuel, Ham and Rose—the ones left behind—huddled together like refugees from an unthinkable war. In their weakened and grief-stricken state they were no match for the implacable Jaggs. When they heard that he and his troglodytic assistants were closing in on them, they chased off along Deep Kill Creek seeking escape from the inevitable.

His hand shaking, Harmony listened gravely for the final section of the corporal's account. It centered, not surprisingly, on the hate-filled Jaggs.

The witch-finder had bloodhounds whose molten barks flowed like lava through the swamp, and their after sunset yowls set the night ablaze. Swearing by his tattered copy of Malleus Maleficarum (Hammer of Witches), Jaggs burned our barn and another outbuilding. His frustration with those who chose not to share his devil-rejecting dogma knew no bounds. The necessary corollary to that frustration was not a superficial doing-God's-will but rather an amoral, murderous rage, against which we were helpless. His brand of violence was inexorable.

We soon exhausted what little magic we possessed.

We were captured and tortured. I can still hear the screams of Rose. My God! And then we were led to a quartet of makeshift gallows in a marshy field behind the dark man's property.

The noose scratched at my neck.

As my last words, I uttered a plea to Ham and Rose and Uncle Samuel that they somehow forgive me. They returned my plea with declarations of love.

Jaggs hanged us.

But he did not destroy us.

For in that chilly dawn—our final dawn—a warm silence connected our spirits.

Our hearts beat as one.

Writing that final sentence, Harmony could not stop a flow of tears. He sobbed, his body wracked with a sorrow he could not even comprehend.

He slept.

When next he opened his eyes, he experienced an unexpected rush of joy: there it was—on his writing table near the burned down candle and the mysterious black bottle.

A large stack of sheets of paper.

The holograph of *The Fable in the Deep.*

He trembled at the sight of it, and then, to himself, he whispered, "We did it. We did it."

Feeling the presence of Corporal Darkester, he raised his fists in jubilation and exclaimed loudly, "We did it! We did it! Your book is written!"

He sensed that the good corporal was very pleased.

A moment of splendor, a moment of warmth came and went.

But, of course, the ghostly entity could not stay—his task had been completed. And yet for Harmony there was more. He saw things left behind under the writing table. He experienced waves of puzzlement as he lifted each of three objects up onto his writing surface next to the manuscript.

A *frisson* coursed through him.

A nervous bubble of saliva formed on his lips.

Were these talismans? Were they tokens of thanks? Were these cryptic reminders of an incredible, incomprehensible experience?

The first was Rose's copy of the poetical works of Lord Byron—a thin, red ribbon marked the page on which the text of "The Prisoner of Chillon" began. The other two objects were bluntly macabre: the bloody knife that Lily had used to plunge through the heart of Shuggart and the mummified paw of Lucifer violently removed by Japonica.

Harmony touched each object as if it were a holy relic.

He drank two celebratory glasses of wine, and then he collapsed onto his cot and slept the sleep of the dead.

In the middle of the night he was awakened by a torch of fire.

Beware the flames! Beware the flames!

Harmony's shriek of despair could be heard in the most remote part of Nahollo Swamp, and though he tried valiantly, he could not save the burning manuscript.

The Fable in the Deep, engulfed in flames, was quickly destroyed.

Harmony stared in disbelief.

How? What? Who?

But with several more moments of reflection, he knew.

He *knew*.

Fists balled at his sides, he pitched his head back and roared,

"Sister Chaos! My sister! Be gone from here! You devil, be gone!"

He sank to his knees. His anguish swallowed him.

Bitterness coating his words, he whispered as if from a dungeon deep within in himself, "I hate you, my sister. I hate you for this."

THE STRANGE CASE
OF BROTHER HARMONY
AND SISTER CHAOS

In the calm of a cool, wet autumn morning, Harmony struggled free of invisible webs of grief. Seemingly without emotion, he gathered up the objects connected to the witches of Nahollo and placed them in a leather pouch. Into a separate pouch he brushed the blackened remnants of *The Fable in the Deep*. He put the black bottle on the counter next to his wood-burning stove.

Momentarily he stood still listening for Corporal Darkester, for he was not fully convinced that the phantom chronicler had left for good. Hearing nothing, he went to do what he must do. He carried an axe and a murderous intention. At the door to the room of Sister Chaos he demanded that she appear before him. When she did not respond, he raised the axe; he felt that to crash open the barrier would be a gladsome experience. But then he paused. He reached out for the doorknob.

And the door swung open on its own.

Peering into the small room he was shocked to find nothing among its nothingness.

Absolutely no sign that any living soul had ever occupied it.

Dust and cobwebs layered every inch of the space.

The odor of the room's emptiness staggered him.

Returning to his area of the shack, he drank a bottle of wine.

Twilight seemed to arrive before noon. Time was out of joint.

He lit a candle and stood away from it, positioning himself just outside of its ragged, glowing circle. And he waited for what wanted to come.

Small in stature and cloaked in shadows, Sister Chaos rose from the approach of night and laid her hand upon her heart. She wore a black robe, head to foot. He could hear her teeth grate. He cleared his throat and said, "Why didn't you stay dead?"

The ensuing silence pressed down upon the scene.

When she did not respond, he said, "Have you hated me because I lived and you didn't?"

Then he shook his head in disgust, for his words sounded banal and trite and beneath the mystery of her.

He sighed, and his tone acquired a gnomic quality.

"What are you going to do? I've asked you to leave. You're no longer welcome. You destroyed something that meant a great deal to me."

A dreadful smile tricked out the corners of her mouth, though the shadows almost hid it. He watched as she nodded. The gesture unsettled him. There was a coolness about her as she moved forward so that he could see her face—or was it *his*?—a suddenly ugly face as if it were deformed in some way he could not fully detect.

Anger sleeved his hands and wrists.

"I want you gone! God damn it, I don't even want you to *exist!*"

Hard upon those words she issued a horrid cry, not human, not animal. She stared at him, her eyes aflame. Her mouth remained open. Her face began to swell, a hideous morphing that caused Harmony to lift his arms in front of him protectively.

She charged at him.

His soul sickened, and he screamed as if he were innocent prey to her predation; she slammed into him between his stomach and his heart. Then the incomprehensible: the essence of her began to shrink into a ball of claws; she burrowed readily, painfully through his flesh and bone. He was knocked flat on his back and sensed that whatever had been Sister Chaos had disappeared completely within him.

He felt as if he had been hit with cannon shot.

He couldn't move.

He couldn't speak.

The twin of his being beat within him like a second heart.

The better part of two days passed before the taste of blood woke him.

Barely able to breathe, he whispered, "Help me. Someone please help me."

Another day passed before Dog Hobble, sensing once again that his friend needed aid, found the spiritualist on the brink of death.

"Conjure man, shit, what's gone on here?"

In a parable of care, Dog stayed with him, nursed him as best he could. Saw to it that he ate a few mouthfuls of biscuit sopped in warm milk or sometimes in honey or syrup. Had him drink lots of water. Helped him up to piss when necessary.

"I ain't gone let you die, man. I just ain't."

Dog's face swirled above Harmony's eyes like a swarm of gnats. He worked his mouth to speak, his throat clicking, his tongue having forgotten how to function. But finally words slowly dribbled out of him.

"I need a fucking miracle," he said.

Despite himself, Dog chuckled.

"You got that right."

Harmony reached for him. Gripped his elbow.

"Dog, help me concentrate. Petition—I got to petition for spiritual help."

"Conjure man, shit, that's not really my thing, but I'll try."

Hours passed. Friend to friend they survived the night and a day of rain and chillier temperatures. It's impossible to know for certain, but a psychic symbiosis of some sort must have emerged.

And then Harmony slept such a deep sleep that Dog, fearing the worse, woke him after five or six hours.

"Conjure man—doncha go leavin' on me. Y'hear?"

Struggling back to consciousness, Harmony blinked his eyes.

"I'm not gone," he muttered, grinning.

Dog stared at him.

"What the fuck, man? You smilin'? Shit, what's goin' on?"

Harmony nodded.

"We got to try somethin'. I had a visitor. A phantom."

"You thinkin' straight?"

"I am." Then he pulled Dog to him as if to command his attention. "There's a black bottle over on the counter. Bring it to me."

Dog laughed nervously.

"Jesus, you think hooch is gone save you?"

Harmony shook his head.

"It's from Old Ways. Corporal Darkester, he…. Never mind, just bring the bottle and give me some room."

Dog hesitated, but when Harmony cursed at him, he obeyed.

On his cot, Harmony chugged it down and closed his eyes.

Both of them waited.

Within a minute, Harmony began to sweat profusely. He squirmed and wallowed as if in pain. Dog hovered there help-lessly. Then Harmony pitched up forward and pointed.

"I see all the demons in the world!" he shouted, pointing as if at some hideous hallucination.

Dog tried to hold him, but Harmony pushed him aside.

He began to vomit violently, choking on the flow. Frightened, Dog moved away from him as he stood shakily, still retching, his arms folded over his stomach.

Then a final, terrible puking.

A black, amorphous mass the size of a softball splattered onto the floor.

It briefly flamed and sizzled before simmering into silence.

Harmony collapsed to his knees.

Dog went to him and held him, and his friend shook as if he were freezing to death.

It took several more days for a semblance of normalcy to return.

"I'm shet of her," Harmony explained to his companion.

"You mean that thing you had me toss in the bayou—*that* was Sister Chaos?"

Harmony nodded.

"It was. I sincerely believe it was."

"Jesus. What a fucking nightmare," Dog murmured.

Harmony narrated the circumstances involving his automatic writing sessions and the manuscript of *The Fable in the Deep* which Sister Chaos had vindictively destroyed. He explained that Corporal Darkester had responded to his petition for help. The black bottle contained a drink, an elixir, not unlike the famous Cherokee "black drink," but Samuel Darkester had altered the ingredients to give his version the capacity to expel evil spirits.

"Sister Chaos turned bad on me—I don't know why exactly. One of those things we just can't know."

Dog breathed out as if his hold on reality were being challenged.

"I don't understand any of this." He hesitated. Fixed his eyes on his friend and added, "What now? You gone keep at this business?"

"No, sir," said Harmony. "I'm carryin' myself away from it. Back to somethin' normal. I'll try my hand at construction work in Sweet River. A whole new life." He grinned at Dog. "You gone have to be keeper of Nahollo Swamp now. Take over for me, OK?"

"Shit, yes, if that's what you think's best."

"I do, sir. I do."

They shook hands.

Drank some hard liquor, though Harmony went easy on it.

Said goodbye.

Friends.

Maybe forever.

He left the shack to Dog.

Decided to hang on to his CDs and CD player. After all, a man who's lived through the 1950s can't live without Chuck Berry, Bo Diddley and Little Richard.

There wasn't much else to do but go and tell Chosen his plan.

On a warm morning he sat outside and watched the sun

spotlight turtles as they positioned themselves to heat up their cold blood. Gators swam desultorily. Egrets winged over the bayou like traces of angels. Once or twice he thought he heard a distant buzzing; the sound generated both a smile and a chill— were those giant wasps of legend stirring out there?

He sipped coffee and thought about what he was leaving behind.

Across the bayou he spotted a raccoon that might have been Maybelline.

He let himself sink into memories, hoping for an inner realm salvation.

He thought about the strange women he'd try to help: Sway de Rille and the others. He thought of Moy and his Neolithic tribe; he thought of the Orpheus boys and the Alligator Man and the Gresham brothers. He thought of Corporal Darkester and a trio of witches, the things they left behind and a book that would never be published. He thought of Sister Gresham.

He remembered that he needed to say goodbye to Took.

Then tears rose behind his eyes.

Another thing: he needed to say goodbye to the ghost of Aidan.

The Kid.

His beloved kid.

And he needed to forget Sister Chaos.

As the sun swung higher, brighter, warmer, he suddenly felt cold inside.

A chilly wind gusted around his heart.

Holy God, what is it?

He dashed to his johnboat and began, furiously, to pole himself to Chosen's. Something was wrong. Very wrong.

He crushed her tear-ravaged face against his shoulder.

"How bad is it, sweetheart? Don't hold nothin' back. Tell it all."

Quivering like a frightened dog, she wailed until he shook her free, gritted his teeth and exclaimed, "Damn it, all, what is it? Say it, sweetheart."

Over wracks of sobbing she said, "My girls."

And Harmony felt his chest go hollow.

Violet and Viola had been missing since late evening of the night before. They'd gone out with a lantern to listen to owls, one of their favorite things to do. But they had not returned.

Holding Chosen by the shoulders, Harmony peered into her face.

"I'll find 'em, sweetheart. I will. I'll do it. I'll bring 'em home safe again."

She muttered things incomprehensible as Harmony sought, immediately, to get a psychic read on things. She and two of her co-workers led him to where they thought the girls had gone.

"I won't fail you," he said to her. "I'll break body and soul for you. For them. I promise. I promise."

But he felt a frozen snake uncoiling in the pit of his stomach. The signs of things looked extremely bleak.

In a copse of pines he got down on one knee. Chosen's hand rested on his shoulder. He concentrated. Saw a flash or two of colored ribbons. Got to his feet, and even as he did he realized that he could never leave the kinds of tasks that continued to be handed to him. There would be no new life.

He embraced Chosen.

"I'll bring 'em back," he whispered. "I will."

He adjusted his top hat and steeled himself.

And as the sun speared through the pines, he went forth into the darkness of the promise he had made.

ABOUT THE AUTHOR

Stephen Gresham has been publishing commercial fiction since 1982. Visit www.stephengresham.com for more details about his publications and writing career.

Stephen also enjoys hearing from readers at greshsl@auburn.edu.

Curious about other Crossroad Press books?
Stop by our site:
http://store.crossroadpress.com
We offer quality writing
in digital, audio, and print formats.